A MESSAGE FOR THE EMPEROR

Also by Mark Frutkin

FICTION

Fabrizio's Return (2006)
Slow Lightning (2001)
The Lion of Venice (1997)
In the Time of the Angry Queen (1993)
Invading Tibet (1991)
Atmospheres Apollinaire (1988)
The Growing Dawn (1983)

POETRY

Iron Mountain (2001)
Acts of Light (1992)
The Alchemy of Clouds (1985)

NON-FICTION

Colourless Green Ideas Sleep Furiously
Short Essays and Alternative Versions (2012)

Walking Backwards
Grand Tours, Minor Visitations, Miraculous Journeys
and a Few Good Meals (2011)

Erratic North
A Vietnam Draft Resister's Life in
the Canadian Bush (2008)

October 2012

A Message
for the
Emperor

To Gary & Cheryl

MARK FRUTKIN

*Best Wishes,
Mark*

ESPLANADE
Books

THE FICTION SERIES AT VÉHICULE PRESS

Published with the generous assistance of The Canada Council for the Arts and the Canada Book Fund of the Department of Canadian Heritage.

Esplanade Books editor: Andrew Steinmetz
Cover design: David Drummond
Photograph of author: Sandra Russell
Set in Adobe Minion by Simon Garamond
Printed by Marquis Book Printing Inc.

Copyright © Mark Frutkin 2012
Dépôt légal, Bibliothèque nationale du Québec and the National Library of Canada, third trimester 2012
All rights reserved.

LIBRARY AND ARCHIVES CANADA CATALOGUING IN PUBLICATION

Frutkin, Mark, 1948-
A message for the emperor : a novel / Mark Frutkin.

ISBN 978-1-55065-336-6

1. Title.

PS8561.R84M48 2012   C813'.54   C2012-903074-0

Published by Véhicule Press, Montréal, Québec, Canada
www.vehiculepress.com

Distribution in Canada by LitDistCo
www.litdistco.ca

Distribution in the U.S. by Independent Publishers Group
www.ipgbook.com

Printed in Canada on FSC certified paper.

*For my father, Reynold Joseph Frutkin,
in his 100th year, and my father-in-law,
Lou Seltzer, in memory.*

List of Characters

A Curator of Chinese Art

Li Wen, a Chinese painter of the Song dynasty – 13th C.
(Style name: Ink Mountain)

Fu Wei, his painting master (Style name: One Tooth)

Ling, a farm wife

A hermit monk

Xu Ming, Li Wen's peasant companion

Zhi, chief of the bandits

Hong, drunken bandit

Ying, girl captured by the bandits

Kuan, abbot of a mountain monastery

Yang Su, scholar and minister in city of Linan

Lady Yang, Yang Su's wife

Po Cheng, Court eunuch, official painter,
and confidant of the Emperor

Emperor Duzong, 15th emperor of the Song dynasty

Jia Sidao, First Minister of the Court

NOTE

Traditionally, Chinese names are written using the family name first and the given name last.

Chuang-tzu dreams that he is a butterfly. When he awakes he asks himself if he is a man who has dreamt that he was a butterfly, or is he now a butterfly dreaming that he is a man?

[Autumn]

Kingfisher Brocades

THE CURATOR OF CHINESE ART swings open the door of his office at the museum, notes with surprise that the new paintings have arrived, places his take-out coffee on a corner of his desk and pries off the lid. He stares at the coffee a moment – *brown as the sound of a cello* – refusing to look up, in an attempt to delay gratification at the arrival of the long-awaited paintings.

He notices a message, unsigned, waits on his desk. Picking it up, he reads: *No room in storage for these at the moment. I installed them here for the time being, figured you wanted them close by.*

Finally, lifting his gaze, he considers the paintings – four Chinese landscapes – that hang down like banners from the ceiling. Spring, on the far left, ripples from an unseen air current.

Four Seasons in China by the Song Dynasty artist Li Wen comes with an intriguing provenance that caught the curator's attention when he first heard the story. The paintings were recorded in the Imperial Catalogue of 1275, a thick volume which held a complete inventory of the Chinese Emperor's artistic holdings. A later catalogue from the Ming Dynasty failed to include them. Somehow the paintings were lost, likely due to the chaos that followed the arrival of the Mongol armies in the south of China during the late thirteenth century. And lost they had remained until rediscovered the previous year rolled up inside a bamboo tube in the basement of a Chinese antique dealer's in old Chinatown. Surprisingly well-preserved, each painting is exactly twenty-two inches in width by forty-eight in length.

The curator opens the top drawer of his desk and removes a rectangular magnifying glass, its handle cross-hatched. He paces back and forth, considering the paintings, the magnifying glass in his right hand. He longs to examine them in detail, to explore their worlds, to wander freely through those landscapes. Pulling his chair close, he settles before the painting of spring and begins.

By mid-morning, the curator's arm has grown tired of holding the magnifying glass. He decides to switch to a more powerful lens. For close-up work he sometimes uses goggles with eye-socket loupes, a type favoured by jewellers. These he can wear mounted on his head, leaving his hands free. He finds the loupes provide an astonishing clarity.

Returning to the painting of spring, the curator delves back into the mountains, deep into their crags, crevices and ravines. Easing his way through shaded forests and gorges, he climbs twisting paths. He enters and begins crossing the broad valley laid out before him, divided into rice paddies. Through the long afternoon he wanders. By early evening, he is alone in the museum, lost in the never-ending forests of China.

Removing the goggles for a moment, he twists his head around – trying to loosen his neck muscles. Replacing the headset, he leans forward in his chair, focusing now on the landscape of autumn.

At the foot of a mountain, next to a multi-fingered lake, stands an open-sided pavilion surrounded by cassia trees. He can smell their faint evergreen-cinnamon scent. Inside the pavilion he sees a man – *he's bald so he must be a monk* – sitting and talking to someone unseen. On a low lacquered table before the monk rests a cup of tea. With exquisite precision and subtlety, the artist has depicted the twisting thread of steam from the cup of tea as it drifts up into the mountains and forms a trail beneath the mist-shrouded trees, a thin grey line winding through patches of mountain spruce, larch, pine and oak.

He notices a figure walking along this trail with what appears to be an oversized load upon his back. At first the curator guesses the image is a woodsman bearing a heap of firewood but when he increases the power on the magnifying loupes, he realizes it isn't firewood at all but a bulky, laden pack. Something straight and narrow with a furred end sticks up from its side.

The curator leans back in his chair. *A brush*, he whispers aloud, *it's a brush*.

~

Li Wen hiked along the trail, the loaded pack weighing heavier and heavier as he climbed through the autumn mountains. Already half the leaves on the maples and oaks had fallen, and the pines and spruce grew darker with each passing day, with each night of lavish frost. As he tramped the path, Wen felt as if something was watching him from behind. Turning, he glanced back the way he had come. The previous day a hunter had told him that tigers were known to haunt these mountains. His heart thumping in his ears, he noticed back along the trail a patch of mottled bamboo shivering in a breeze. But he saw no sign of an animal. Breathing deeply and sighing, he trudged on.

Again he paused, gazed back into the forest, into the tops of the towering pines, and the river of blue silk sky high above. Suddenly everything felt upside down, as if the slit above was a rough stream rushing through a heavily wooded gorge. White mist drifted from the pines. With the vision of the mist came the memory of his master in the pavilion at the monastery. Everything that Li Wen knew about calligraphy and painting he had learned from his master, Fu Wei.

Wen's last meeting with his master had taken place three days earlier. It had begun like a hundred previous sessions. That afternoon, however, Master Wei's cup of tea seemed to be emitting an unusual amount of steam. Wen considered that the steam from his own cup appeared rather meagre by comparison.

Wen had initiated the conversation: "One day I feel I am the greatest painter of the South and the next I believe I have never executed a single true stroke. I fear I must leave this place. It seems as if I have been doing the same painting over and over for the past two years."

Master Wei nodded.

Fu Wei was a man of average height and stocky build, but he seemed larger than life, solid and immovable, with a core of iron. And yet, at times it struck Wen that Master Wei was hardly there at all, as if he could pass his hand right through him.

Fu Wei's style name was One Tooth. *How does one gain a sobriquet like One Tooth?* Wen wondered, not for the first time. *Especially as he seems to have most of his teeth but, in fact, has only one eye.*

Li Wen continued his complaint. "I must leave. I am learning nothing here. I am the worst of students."

Master Wei took a sip of tea, nodded again, said nothing.

"Perhaps because I am the worst of students, I am giving you a reputation as the worst of teachers."

Fu Wei spoke: "I don't require a student to make me a teacher."

Wen persisted: "But what am I doing here?"

Wei countered with a question, as he often did. "What do *you* think?"

Their interviews were always like this, the push and pull, the struggle to arrive somewhere. *But where?*

Wen answered: "I don't know. I just feel that I must leave. I believe I can learn nothing more here."

Master Wei nodded, remained silent.

"I have drunk a thousand cups of tea in this room and today I feel as if I have learned nothing."

This time, One Tooth did not nod, but sipped from his cup, his single eye piercing as he looked at his student. Finishing his tea, he turned his cup upside down on the low table. "You are correct. Our work together is done."

Despite his current difficulties, Li Wen felt profound gratitude toward the teacher who long ago had lifted him up from his previous life. At that time, Wen was barely surviving by poling passengers back and forth across the nearby river in his small boat. One day, nine years earlier, his only passenger had been Fu Wei, the one-eyed abbot from the local monastery.

Once the abbot had taken his seat in the boat, he said to Li Wen: "You look as if you are about to weep, my friend."

It was true. Wen's father, a fisherman and a devout Buddhist, had drowned the previous month and Wen felt crushed by grief.

His mother had died giving birth to him, her first and only child. Raised by his father, Wen spent his childhood going from shore to shore in the boat. Later, he took the pole from his father's hands and he himself became a boatman. He loved the constant motion, and felt there was something symbolic about it. For Buddhists, reaching the far shore meant the attainment of enlightenment – but, in Wen's case, every time he reached the other side, he turned around and went back. Perhaps not out of a fear of failure but a fear of success. He wondered. Or maybe he saw the value of returning for other passengers wishing to cross the river. It was his livelihood, after all.

That day, Wen and the abbot had crossed in silence.

"Come see me in the monastery," Fu Wei had said, stepping onto the far shore and slipping a coin into the boatman's hand.

Wen had come, and stayed on, and with One Tooth's help over the next several years, he had been educated, learning to read and write. As for calligraphy, the brush felt natural in his hand. Once he had attained a certain level of skill at writing the characters, his master had allowed him to begin the study of painting and poetry. Despite living in the monastery, Wen had never taken vows as a monk. And the abbot had never insisted.

Now Wen was thinking of leaving. He repeated, "I must go away from this place. I long to wander, to see the world."

Master Wei nodded. "I understand. The time is right. I would like you to deliver a message for me." One Tooth had reached into his robes and removed a hollow segment of bamboo, about a thumbnail in diameter and a single handspan in length. It was as if he had been waiting for this moment. As he spoke to Wen, he leaned forward, holding the bamboo in the fingers of both hands horizontally before him.

Master Wei said, "This bamboo contains a message...a message for the Emperor."

"The Emperor?" Wen hesitated to take the segment of bamboo hovering before him. He simply stared at it.

The master nodded. "Yes. There have been serious developments in the capital recently, and I wish to get a message to the Son of Heaven. It must be delivered only to him, directly into his hands. The message is for the Emperor's eyes alone. I want you to deliver it."

"It could take me a year to reach the Imperial Court. There are faster ways to convey an urgent message to the Emperor. Why send it with me?" Although he did not want to show it, Wen was shaking inside with fear – not at the journey, which would surely be dangerous, but at the harrowing responsibility of delivering a message to the Emperor. He felt as if he had just stepped off a cliff – or been pushed. Wen took a deep breath and continued. "Half a dozen chains of mountains block the way between here and there. There will be wild rivers to cross. Innumerable dangers."

"Yes, that is true. It is a great distance to the capital of Linan and the Emperor's Court. In any case, if you travel well, the message will reach the Emperor at the proper time. Its premature arrival would be disastrous." One Tooth paused. "As would its arriving too late."

Wen felt he had no choice. This was perhaps his last test from Fu Wei. He took the bamboo with a bow of his head. Holding it with the tips of his fingers, he stared at it, wondering what his master wished to communicate to the Emperor.

"I suggest you leave before the new moon. It will take a year, as you say. On your journey, you shall create four paintings, one for each season. These you will present on your arrival at the Court in Linan as a long-life gift to the Emperor – my good wishes for his longevity."

"A full year of walking and painting. A full scroll of seasons."

Wen turned, gazed toward the mountains, then faced Master Wei again. "Though this journey intrigues me, it fills me with fear. It will present many difficulties. Who am I to deliver a message to the Emperor? How will I gain entry to the Court?"

"It is good that you hesitate, for it will not be an easy task."

Wen waited for Fu Wei to go on. After a moment's silence, Wen said, "It will be a long time before I see you again."

Master Wei paused. "I believe our work together is finished. You will not be back this way again."

From the distance came the sound of washerwomen pounding silk on blocks along the river.

With his one eye, Master Wei stared at Wen and then turned away.

∼

As he climbed the mountain trail, Wen recalled the look in that single eye – fierce, wise, filled with sorrow. The other eye, as always, had been sealed shut.

The path levelled off for a ways, skirted a pool, then climbed again, a sparkling brook splashing down alongside the trail. The water was pure and clear, the air scented with the resin of pine needles that carpeted the pathway. When Wen came to a steeper stretch, the straps of his pack, woven of light but sturdy hemp, dug into his shoulders. The weight made him feel like an insect bearing a load twice its own size despite the fact that he had brought only the essentials.

First, he had packed the painter's Four Treasures: paper, brushes, ink sticks and an inkstone.

As for brushes, he had chosen numerous types of various sizes. Each lightweight bamboo handle held hairs of a different animal: weasel, horse, deer, goat. He included a brush of rabbit hair for painting swirling streams (it was said that he painted streams with such precision that the viewer could hear the sound of water flowing), and another from the breast feathers of the pihi bird, to reveal the thousand versions of snow. And, finally, the wolf hair brush for painting the peaks of the highest mountains.

Plus one brush that never touched ink. The tiny bamboo brush had a tip assembled of dozens of silk strands gathered together. Each time he would begin a painting, he would hold this brush above a blank sheet of paper, twirling it lightly in a figure eight while his head emptied – and then filled with images. Mountains and streams beyond measure would arise from the charged emptiness of the page.

It was like the spirit of a child drawn to the womb in which it would be born.

The paper that Wen had packed – the second of the four treasures – was fashioned by an ancient method from old fishing nets. Wen had taken four of the dried sheets of paper, laid them on top of each other, rolled them tight and inserted them into a hollow bamboo. He had also packed sheets of thin rice paper for sketching, rolled into another bamboo.

To these treasures he added a number of black ink sticks and a grinding stone made of turtle shell. In a cloth wrapper, he packed a final ink stick that was a gift from One Tooth. It was made of burnt pine and glue and powdered pearl, and had been aged for over a hundred years. As well, he added his artist's seal, a small jade with the character depicting his style name carved into one end, and a tiny pot that held a paste of scarlet cinnabar consisting of ground silk and oils.

The pack was also weighed down with a sack of rice, a bag of dried tea leaves, a packet of salt, a single cooking pot, a bowl and a spoon, a fire-making kit, two thin but warm blankets and a few pieces of clothing, including a padded jacket for the coldest weather. He added a string of copper coins, as well as three small pieces of silver, another gift from Fu Wei. These latter were sewn into the lining of the pack along with three sheets of 'flying money', accredited receipts which could be cashed in larger towns along the way, and two paper notes, worth twenty strings of eighty cash coins each, given to him at the master's behest by the monastery. The paper notes, made from the bark of the paper mulberry tree, bore the inscription: "Counterfeiters will be decapitated."

Finally, he added the narrow bamboo that carried the message for the Emperor. At first he thought he would sew it into the bottom of his pack with the silver pieces but at the last minute he decided to hide the message in plain sight. Uncurling the message, he removed it from the bamboo – for a fleeting moment he was tempted to read it but resisted –and hid it in the hollow handle of his tiny silk-strand brush.

Stopping to rest, Wen unhitched himself from the pack and set it on the ground. He wiped his brow and gazed out toward the distant valley behind him, a jade green ocean descending in waves and swells of trees. Untying a gourd that hung from his belt, Wen drank water from the stream, and sat. A troop of monkeys gambolling in a stand of pines raised a ruckus over his presence. Ahead, the path curved into deeper-shadowed forest and climbed toward the first crest of mountains, towering crags in the distance, the highest, snow-capped. He knew he would not be able to cross directly over the loftier peaks, but would be forced to spend weeks skirting around the rocky heights.

In at least one place, he had learned it would be necessary to travel over a snow-covered pass. Wen dreaded this part of the journey – he sensed it would be extremely difficult and dangerous. Fishing out a rudimentary map covering the first portion of his journey, he sought again the name of the distant town where he hoped to spend the winter. There was much walking to be done if he was to reach the town before the snows came. To take his mind off the struggles which he knew awaited him, he vowed to begin the autumn painting within the next few days.

Wen rested, pondering the stream at his feet, its flow never ceasing. Taking out a sheet of rice paper and a piece of charcoal, he sketched the stream with its immersed pebbles, its weedy edge, its glistening ripples. His hand slipped quickly over the sheet as he reflected. *A stream includes innumerable, ever-changing qualities: twists and turns, sparkling water, stones in its bed, water plants along the edge, the sounds of gurgling and bubbling. It may have a beginning and an end but these are impossible to fix. Upstream, there may be a place where it springs out of the earth; downstream, a point where it joins another stream or even slips into the sea. Once it joins the sea, then which is the water of stream and which the water of ocean?*

He glanced back the way he had come. *The trail too is like a stream. When did I truly begin on this path? Three days ago? Years earlier when I first met Wei? What of the path that led me to Master Wei, and the path before that? The self, too, is a stream – it cannot be fixed, cannot be described in final terms as this or that. It can be named, but what is a name but a cluster of sounds, the stream gurgling? And yet, and yet –* he stared at the water, finishing the final few strokes of the sketch: *there is a stream, there is a path. Stream, no stream; path, no path; self, no self – this ambiguity is our life.*

Immersed in the silence of his reverie, Wen heard a sudden noise in the brush. He leapt to his feet, knife in hand, imagining a tiger descending on him in mid-leap. But it was only a medium-sized brown bird that emerged from the bushes and hopped onto a low branch. For the rest of his journey, Wen kept his knife handy. Tucked inside the cord that served as his belt, it shone in the sunlight.

The world fell away behind him. Other than several curious and annoying troops of monkeys that had screeched at his earlier passing and the dozen in the nearby trees currently complaining about his presence, he hadn't seen anyone today except for a pair of woodcutters who had given him an astonished look when he tried to explain that he was headed to the capital to see the Emperor.

Wen recognized them as the poorest of the poor by their clothing of mulberry bark. The woodcutters were simple, friendly men who had seen little of the world. The one with a high flat forehead commented, "The Emperor lives with the Immortals in Heaven. You cannot walk these trails to Heaven."

The other with the missing finger warned, "Tigers have been seen in recent days. Passing through these mountains is not safe. Come share food with us. We have monkey meat and rice wine. We would appreciate your company in this month of the Cold Dew. No sense freezing, sleeping outdoors under the shivering hare of an autumn moon. I have never been to the city in the valley and would like to hear your tales."

But the hike to the hut of the two men would have taken Wen half a day out of his way, so he thanked them, but refused their generous invitation.

Before the woodcutters left, they gave Wen a gift. A crude mask of mulberry bark with eyeholes cut in it. "Wear the mask on the back of your head while you walk. The tiger only attacks from behind and this will confuse him. And if you see a tiger approaching through the forest, cover your ears, for the tiger's roar can paralyze a man, making your escape impossible." With that, they dissolved into the forest, their own bark masks gazing back at him as they dissappeared.

"I am truly alone," Wen said aloud, still staring at the dappled forest where the two brothers had vanished.

Truth be told, he gloried in his solitude. The life of a hermit had always appealed to him after spending his early years on the boat and in the alleys and taverns of the city, and after living in the crowded monastery. To go days and weeks with nothing but the wind to listen to and nothing to see but mountains, mist, clouds, sunrises and sunsets was splendid. A calling bird was all he needed for friendship. He would happily learn the language of brooks and would count the shivering of leaves as gestures and greetings from the natural world. Perhaps, like one of the Ancients, he would forget his own name and find his way to immortality over the Western mountains.

But, for now, he had work to do, an exacting task to accomplish. He had no doubt that the paintings for the Emperor and the journey to Linan were a final test from his teacher. The responsibility of delivering the message weighed on his mind. *How will I find the Emperor? How will I obtain an audience with him?* Fu Wei had given him the name of an important official in the capital but how would he find this man and would the official meet with him and agree to help him?

Whenever he abandoned these worries, Wen found the crisp, fresh mountain air invigorating, and the grandness of the undertaking before him filled him with energy. As he walked he watched carefully but with light-hearted ease, awaiting the arrival of scenes that could be included in the painting of autumn, meanwhile trying to ignore his aching feet and the worrisome thought of tigers at the back of his mind. When he reached the end of a thick stand of spruce, he stepped out to the edge of an abyss and considered the view over mountains and valleys, shadows cutting and carving into the forests below. Yet it wasn't right, it wasn't yet the inspiration he needed to start the painting.

Wen realized that it was growing dark, the temperature dropping fast. The sun melted behind the western peaks. Leaning his pack up against a pine tree, he started to gather together long soft pine needles that covered the forest floor. In a few minutes, he had piled together a tumulus of needles. This would serve as his bedding for the night. Removing his blankets from the pack, he rolled up in them, and nestled underneath the huge resinous pile. Reaching out, he tugged his pack next to his body. *In the morning I will start a fire, cook rice and make tea. For water, I have the brook that continues to mirror the trail. Perhaps tomorrow I will find a view worthy to inspire a painting for the Emperor.*

Staring into the fading light of the heavens, he wondered again about Fu Wei's message to the Emperor. For a moment, he thought he could read it in the sky, in the characters of a drifting cloud, but then night came on, ink spilling across the heavens, soaking into silk, dousing the dusk. His own heat warmed the cocoon as he stretched out and relaxed. The sky above the trees turned a rich black and a hundred thousand stars sparkled like dew hanging from the tips of pine boughs. For a while, he lay on his back watching bats tack through the tree branches above. Then came the sound of a distant roar deep in the forest, but he was too tired to care.

As he fell asleep with his hand resting on the hilt of his knife, he sensed, with the clarity and conviction of an infant recognizing the face of its own mother, that he would, the next morning, awake in another's dream.

∼

Wen awoke to sunlight in his eyes, the peculiar visible silver light that drifts down through a pine forest, filtered through open fans of needles. To a chorus of trilling birds, he rolled from his cocoon, breathing scarves of mist in the chill air.

Wen set about striking a spark into a nest of dry moss. It wasn't difficult. In these high mountains, the world was a dry place. One spark led to another, and another. He added more moss to feed the hungry bird-mouths of the flames; then added small sticks, followed by larger ones. He gazed into the flames and saw that the fire would hold. Digging a bag of rice from his pack, he dumped several handfuls into his pot and headed for the stream.

Kneeling down, Wen untied the gourd from his belt and dipped it in the fresh water. The stream glowed with the slightest resin-yellow luminescence from the pine forests dissolved in its veins. Starting to pour the water from gourd to pot, he stopped. *A fish.* A tiny fish, the length of two of the three sections of his little finger. Pale green, transparent at the edges, it waved its silky diaphanous fins as it swam energetically in circles inside the gourd, flicking its tail.

Lowering the gourd into the stream again, Wen let the water in the gourd join the water of the brook and, with a shiver, the fish swam free. Taking another scoop, he poured the water into his pot and headed back to the fire to begin cooking the rice.

Later, after eating his rice and drinking two cups of strong tea the colour of evergreen shadows, Wen began to load his supplies back into the pack. He recalled again the small bamboo brush that held the letter from his teacher to the Emperor. Taking it from his pack, he sat back and held it, staring, trying to determine the nature of its contents. The warning words of Fu Wei came back to him: "... for the Emperor's eyes alone." No, it was not for him to know the contents and yet he wondered, and continued wondering as he placed the brush back in the pack, loaded the rest of his supplies and started hiking up the trail, the faint howl of gibbons echoing from the forest.

All morning he imagined the letter scrolling open before him. Wondering what it said, he brooded over it for hour after hour until his mind was in pain from the not-knowing of it. And then the rhythm of walking took over and his mind settled and let go of the letter, and he began to notice again where he was, began to note the tallest or most contorted trees, awoke to the occasional views from the trail as it skirted a chasm, the regular steps of falls that punctuated the stream. Twice he stopped and made sketches, using charcoal from that morning's fire: one sketch of a bush filled with orange berries and tiny chittering green birds, and another of an old bent pine curling off the edge of a cliff, seeming to gather the near and distant mountains in its branches.

In late afternoon, recalling the sketches he had made thus far in his journey, he came to a decision. *Tomorrow I will begin the painting, if I find a suitable location and if the weather holds.*

A short while later, as if the heavens had heard his thoughts, the solid blue of the sky was overtaken by bruise-purple clouds. The wind started to gust. He hurried along the trail in hopes of finding a shallow cave or at least an overhang of rock under which he could shelter when the rain came in earnest.

Along the left side of the path, across the stream, the landscape rose sharply. The steep treeless rise covered with low grass then flattened out into an open shaded forest with widely spaced oak trees. In the distance, the forest ended abruptly at a long horizontal wall of stone filled with pocks and crags. He hurried along, eyeing the line where forest met rock. As the first few drops of rain raised puffs of dust along the trail, he sighted a deeper shadow through the trees. Thinking it might be the mouth of a cave, he crossed the stream, hurried up through the woods, smelling the faint sweet rot of fallen leaves, and found a place where the stone wall offered a canopy of granite, a shallow indentation that would provide protection from all but the most tempestuous rains.

Removing his pack, he crawled into the dry pocket just as the skirts of a heavy downpour swept through the trees. He was well protected and set about gathering dry twigs from the margins of the shallow cave for a small fire. Soon he was watching the smoke of his fire hang suspended in the branches of the oaks where it joined the rising mist, while he drank tea and cooked rice, prepared to spend the night listening to the sound of rain ticking through leaves.

The next morning, the rain persisted – not heavily but with a steady 'pat, pat, pat' on the broad leaves nearby. He decided to spend the day in his dry shelter and sketch.

But he didn't start sketching immediately. He knew from experience that such an approach would not work for him. The painting had to be assembled in his mind and let go and reassembled numerous times before he could lift a brush. He had to bring his vision to a place where the brush would move of its own accord and the ink would flow with the ease and naturalness of that stream burbling down the mountain, effortless, sparkling and dark, winding and unwinding in the distance.

Just as brushes should be soaked in warm water before use, he had to soften his mind, let his imagination grow supple and loose and free.

He began by sitting cross-legged on the earth at the edge of his cave, looking out and down. Facing west, he felt his breath flow in and out, in and out again. He let the moist air, the sweet scent of rain and forest, fill his lungs. He breathed out, dissolving into trees and leaves, into the crags and cliffs of the mountains, into sky. And then he breathed the world in again.

Near the corner of the cave entrance, he noticed a rock the size of a deer sitting on its haunches, grey and smooth on top, moss stippling its lower parts. Contemplating the stone, he pictured it as a mountain. And he realized that each mountain for ten thousand *li* in every direction was nothing but these bits of stone built up. A mountain was made of rocks such as this – the stone was in the mountain and, conversely, the mountain was in the stone.

And he saw that he too was not separate from the earth. He was in the mountains and the mountains were in him.

A breeze swayed through the trees, the leaves shimmered and the subtle pattern of light and shadow on the stone's surface flickered and changed.

Unrolling the rice paper, he picked up a chunk of charcoal from the edge of the fire and began to sketch the rock before him. He did not look with his eyes alone, but himself became stone, felt what it was like to be stone, a stone that breathes, both weighing on the earth and weightless. He sat, head bowed, his hand a bird flickering across the page, darting this way and that. Sketch after sketch of the stone appeared before him, until his sketching was like breathing. In this way the day passed.

∼

The sky had emptied itself out. Li Wen, still in his shallow cave, felt the solidity of the earth under him, and gazed out on the world. Above the oaks, the sky was the pale, washed-out blue of autumn, and cool. He started a fire, ate breakfast, packed up his things and returned to the trail.

As he climbed, Wen kept an eye out for a good place to begin the painting. It was an excellent day to work. A steady wind in the night had removed the moisture from the earth. The air was now still and fresh. He sensed that it would not rain again in the next several days.

Around mid-morning, he halted in a small flat clearing that offered an open view over mountains spiking north and east. At one side stood a small pine with a low horizontal branch where he could later drape the finished painting to dry. The stream that had followed the trail for the past three days was not far off.

Wen shrugged the weight from his back and rubbed his neck. After building a fire with pine sticks, he fetched a pot of water and placed it over the flames. While the water heated, he took his turtleshell grinding stone in hand, flicked a couple of drops of streamwater into it and began rubbing a stick of black ink across the inside bottom of the shell. This repetitious action soothed his mind. He made no attempt to consider how he would start the painting but knew, from long experience, that he must let a space open up inside him first. He had the confidence that this space would eventually fill with an image by the time he lifted the first brush.

When he had ground enough pigment – *releasing the dragon* – he tested the temperature of the water on the fire. It had to be warm but not hot. Taking the pot off the flames, he chose his brushes, placing them in the water to soften the bristles. While they soaked, he unrolled the charcoal sketches he had drawn since starting the journey and spread them out on the ground. He then extracted the four pieces of fishing net paper from the bamboo tube, set one aside, and replaced the others.

As he prepared, he heard birds calling in the distance, and noticed the patterns of their cries. He felt a gentle movement of the breeze pass through the spruce forest, curl around a stone promontory and drift lazily past him. He smelled the evergreen resin that perfumed the air. Rolling out the blank paper sheet, he placed eight small stones to hold it down.

As Wen reached out for the brush of silk strands, everything around him slowed further. The silences between bird cries grew vast, the breeze seemed to hold for a moment, the world spacious and still. Light and shadow spattered the trunks of the oaks and maples, drifting along the boles with each subtle murmur of breeze.

A single branch of white pine stretched horizontally over the valley far below, clusters of long green needles like open fans against the silken opalescent blue.

Picking up the brush – its weight almost imperceptible – he raised it to the heavens, horizontal above his gaze. He then bowed to the heavens as well as the blank page as he held the brush over it. He paused, drinking in the radiance and freshness of the blank sheet. It would never be so perfect again. It saddened him that he felt this need to sully its purity.

He paused, the brush hovering over the page. He waited until the empty space within him gave birth to mountains.

Before he knew it, evening was descending. He had spent the entire day painting, grinding more pigment, painting on and on: mountain crags, towering spruce and pines in dark masses of ink, a trail through the forest, a pavilion with a robed monk, and the cavernous valley below with its deep arrows of light and shadow. He had listened to the stream in the distance and let the sound of flowing water inspire the movement of his brush, employing the full arsenal of his art: brushstrokes of bent-ribbon and entangled-firewood, lotus-leaf strokes and ax-cut strokes, strokes of ox hair, water ribbons and ravelled rope.

His breathing was in perfect rhythm with the movement of his brush. He knew he had to dampen his intensity or he would grip the brush too tightly, as he worked both *ch'i* and *yün*, spirit and harmony, into the landscape. (*What matters,* he recalled his teacher saying, *is the vigour of the stroke; vigour joined with delicacy. One needs both energy and gentleness.*) The work took tremendous effort and yet, it was effortless because he was so relaxed, so utterly engaged, at one with the two landscapes before him – one real, one imagined.

As he gazed at the work, he paused on hearing a faint sound. *The roar of an animal. A tiger. Far off, and yet....* A shudder passed through him and he turned to look behind. *Tonight I shall sleep near the fire, one hand on my knife. And when I walk I will continue to wear the mulberry-bark mask the woodcutters gave me.* He tried to put the thought of tigers from his mind.

The next morning, early, he was at it again, and again the sun arced over the canopy of forest as quickly as the passing of a broad-winged bird. He glanced up from the painting, from the intensity of his work, and was shocked to see the grainy light of dusk.

The fine weather continued for a week, and he lost himself in the painting over and over again just as a wandering hermit would happily lose himself in endless mountain landscapes. He slept deep dreamless sleeps, and awoke each morning utterly refreshed. Every daylight hour, he immersed himself completely in the work, thinking of nothing but what was before him. He was one with the brush, the ink, the paper, the mountains. Nothing else existed.

In the end, he was satisfied – when he stepped back and regarded the painting, he saw that it offered as much delight as the actual landscape before him.

After he hung the painting over the pine branch to dry, he succumbed to a delicious fatigue. Sitting relaxed on the ground, he turned his gaze to the valley below. No huts or villages were visible, but in the distance he could distinguish a thin line of smoke, which, for some reason, he found vaguely disquieting.

He cooked rice, ate his fill, and drank tea. He then fell soundly and thoughtlessly asleep under his blankets, the howl of gibbons fading into the forest.

∼

As Wen hiked down the trail, he noticed that the pattern of fallen leaves thick on the ground resembled the kingfisher brocades worn by the wives of rich merchants in his hometown. Wen's daydream was diverted by a particularly large maple leaf that came wafting down before him on the chill autumn wind. *Soon it will snow.* He picked up the pace, the trail descending toward the valley below.

The next day proved sunny and a little warmer. In late morning, Wen came upon an open glade with soft grass up to his knees halfway down the mountain. He removed the autumn painting from its bamboo tube, unrolled it and weighted down the corners with stones as before. Searching in his pack, he found the precious, hundred-year-old ink stick from Wei. While he ground the stick with a few drops of water in the turtle shell, he contemplated the open area in the upper right hand of the painting where he would brush the poem.

When the ink was prepared – though black it glowed with the sheen of pearl in angled light – he took up his smooth, long-pointed calligraphy brush, moistening its bristles a few moments in his mouth. *As if with my own tongue I am teaching the brush to speak.*

Kneeling before the painting, Wen prepared himself. He wasn't thinking about the poem he would write – that would arise from the ink itself, its pearly radiant blackness reflecting the world around him. In any case, it wasn't only the words that mattered. The way he cut the strokes, the action of his brush, his calligraphic style, were just as important to him as the characters of the poem and the painting itself.

He waited a long while. In the sky above, clouds arose, passed and disappeared. They were repeated as pure reflection in the pool of ink in the turtle shell. The mountains and trees too were reflected there, and his own image holding the brush in his hand. He continued kneeling, leaning back, awaiting the right moment. Finally, he moved toward the shell until the brush in his hand touched and fused with the brush reflected in the ink and the two brushes became one.

Dipping the brush, he soaked the bristles. Dipped it again until it was saturated with ink, as if it were so swollen with words the brush had to speak or spill its blood on the earth. Like the water in a waterfall giving in and tumbling over the edge, he leaned into the painting with purpose, entering the landscape itself – the landscape in the painting and the one around him. They were inseparable.

With steady brushstrokes, he wrote the characters in a vertical column on the painting.

With subtle shifts in the pressure and direction of the brush, he ensured his vertical strokes, the *shu*, were planted in the earth and rock of the mountains, while his horizontal *heng* strokes, and the *pie* and *na* diagonals, had the grace and harmony of pine boughs or blades of grass. Each character, written in 'running script', consisted of strokes that held in balance heaven and earth and the man who linked them together. It had to be spontaneous and perfect the first time – no erasures were possible, there was no going back to make corrections.

Leaves on maples blush
At the beauty of the autumn wind

Distant lakes of ink reflect
A pure image of mountains

Each tree a brush swaying in the breeze
Drawing clouds across the heavens.

Wild geese descend in lines to the south
A lone goose wings north

When finished, he cleaned the brush and put it away. He then took out his seal and the tiny pot of red pigment. He enjoyed the faint scratchy sound the porcelain lid made when he slid it off – perhaps because he had come to know it as a sound that suggested his work was near completion, that he had done all he could do, that nothing more could be accomplished. It was the melancholy sound of fulfillment. The cinnabar pigment in the jar resembled a scarlet sea beaten by the wind and frozen in mid-froth. Taking his seal in hand – a smooth, squared jade stone about the size of a thumb – he pressed it into the pot of thick pigment and imprinted the square image onto the painting. He then blew over the character for his style name, breathing it into life.

He replaced the lid on the jar, and packed it away along with his stone seal. For the remainder of that day, he rested, warming himself by the fire, eating rice and drinking tea at his leisure. He read from the only book he had brought – a collection of ancient poems that he contemplated like passing clouds. Occasional sounds intruded on his reverie: gibbons, monkeys, a melancholy songbird calling from the deep forest (*the deeper the shadows, the more luminous the song*), and again, a tiger's roar, distant yet not as distant as before.

The next day dawned bright and fresh, and he began walking early. In late morning, four horsemen approached him along the trail. As they drew near, he counted three soldiers accompanying an official. They halted and looked down at him. "Where are you headed, stranger?" asked the soldier in the lead.

"I am going to the Imperial Court in the capital. I was told by a hunter that this trail would take me in the right direction. Is it true?"

The soldier, incredulous, looked at his fellows and they all shared a hearty laugh. "The capital? You might as well try to reach the Abode of the Immortals over the Western Mountains."

The official spoke crossly to the others, "Do not joke. This might be a spirit testing us, disguised in peasant's clothes."

The first soldier smirked. "He doesn't even have a horse. Anyway, good luck to you, stranger. We must be off."

"My apologies," said the official. "I am District Magistrate Yen and we are in a hurry to arrest a man for filial impiety. We hope to reach his village before he hears of our approach and flees for the mountains. Yes, this road leads in the direction of the capital, but it is a far distance indeed, and few villages come between here and that next range of peaks." He pointed.

Turning his horse to go, he hesitated. "We have reports of tigers. Have you seen any?"

"I have heard them, but seen none."

The riders rode off into the distance and Wen continued on. The rest of that day he saw no one else along the trail. As he hiked deeper and deeper into the forest, exquisite shafts of light pierced the high canopy of thousand-year old pines. Eventually the trail started to climb into dry oak forest. He laboured and sweated, the pack weighing on his back.

Finally the forest thinned and he came to a place where a cliff jutted out high above a valley. To his left, he could see the sun setting over a run of peaks many *li* in the distance. As he felt the temperature begin to drop, he worked out of his pack and plopped down, taking a long drink of water from his jug. *I will make camp here for the night.* He drank again and thought. *I am so deeply into the mountains now, it is as if I am disappearing. That magistrate thought I might be a spirit. Perhaps he was right. I could die on this mountainside and my flesh and bones would join the earth and become the bark of trees, grow into leaves and needles; my blood flow into streams and rivers; my breath become mist rising like incense. Perhaps I am already a ghost.*

That night the moon was full. He would not see another human being along the trail until the round moon had been pared to half.

∽

Continuing to wear the mulberry-bark mask given to him by the woodsmen, Wen half-expected to turn a corner and come face to face with the hot liquid eyes of a tiger. Turning and looking back, he knew there was nothing he could do about it. The tiger would only appear when it was ready to be seen, and not before.

He paused, leaned on his walking stick. Wen mused on how a mountain trail never follows a straight line but twists and turns, dodges this way, feints that way, like a bat stitching and tacking through a high forest. His eyes scanned the sunlit trail ahead where it turned left, climbed slightly and disappeared to the right around a low hill of shattered and tumbled rocks. A few shadows of trees crossed the trail but other than that the path was entirely suffused with light. Then suddenly, as a cloud passed, the path dipped into shadow, and back to light again.

The sky blinked, he thought.

After that everything changed. The landscape came alive. He began to enter the natural world in a different way. He could see the face and tail of the wind. The wind wasn't empty and invisible, but was a being as alive as any clouded leopard or fox curling around a fallen log or slipping into the undergrowth. The shivering pine needles and maple leaves communicated with him, and he recognized that the gurgles of the stream followed a pattern just as in any other language. He sensed the glowing sound the sunlight made when it fell to earth. He heard the animals whispering through the forest, heard the songbird's song as it was ticking and rising in its throat. He sensed the natural order of things, in the earth, in the sky, in the stars of heaven and the patterns of dew on the grass. He wasn't outside the world looking in but was part of the landscape. A joy he had never before experienced lightened his step. The pack felt empty, his body, weightless. Like the shadow of a cloud rippling over the earth, he passed without leaving a footprint.

He turned a corner in the trail and saw an abandoned, half-collapsed hut that awoke a memory in him. It was soon after he had arrived at the monastery. Wen had been out walking and came upon a small silkworm house, an old woman sitting outside on a low bench. She had motioned him over. As he approached, it had struck him. *It's the spirit of my mother.* He sat on the ground before her. She held a shallow wooden tray in her lap. "What are you doing?" he asked.

She explained that she was sorting silkworm cocoons.

"Where does the silk come from?"

"We must begin at the beginning." She described how the silk moths laid eggs on mulberry leaves. The eggs would then hatch into caterpillars that fed on the mulberry. The silkworm caterpillars spewed out a filament from two holes in their heads, an unbroken thread which they wrapped around themselves, turning their heads in a figure-eight motion.

"They wrap themselves in their own cocoons?"

"Yes." She smiled at him and he was touched by the kindness in her face.

She ran her fingers through the cocoons in the tray. "From these I must decide which will live and be allowed to hatch and go on to lay new eggs. The rest will be killed, their cocoons unravelled, and the long threads spun into silk. The unbroken thread from a single cocoon would reach beyond that distant hill." She pointed.

When he left, she said, "I will not see you again," and he had turned away with an overwhelming feeling of sorrow. But not before she had given him a few woven strands of raw silk which he would later cut and gather into a tip for his smallest brush.

～

All day, as Wen walked, he felt the presence of something. The hair on the back of his neck kept standing up and he turned about on the trail constantly to check behind. His fear began to build. He felt watched. It seemed he wasn't simply being stalked by an animal but by a strange powerful entity that embodied the essence, the spirit, of the forest. Sometimes he thought it wasn't his own life he feared for but the inability to accomplish his duty, to fulfill this final task from his Master.

He felt out of sorts, questioning this entire journey and the effort it involved. What was the point? He should have stayed back at the monastery, he told himself. *I never should have left.* The pack felt heavier than ever and his body ached. He felt a weight on his mind, as if some outside force had entered him.

Then his fear would rise and his legs would turn to water. At one point, his fear pitched him into a fever of panic. *The message, the Emperor's message, perhaps it contains a magical incantation for keeping tigers at bay – the Master is testing me to see if I have the resolve, the independence, to go against his admonitions, to reveal the message and, in that bold act of defiance, save my own life.*

Wen came to his senses. *Don't be a fool,* he told himself, *you are being tortured by your own fear.*

He placed his hand on the back of his head and felt the face there. *A man with two faces, going in two directions at once.*

That night, he slept on the ground next to his fire with his hand gripping his knife, an ancient, well-made blade from his father. As the knife was so sharp – his father used to boast that it could slice starlight – he was fearful of cutting himself in his sleep, but he felt he had no choice.

The fire had died out, its comforting crackle having fallen silent. The air was permeated with the smell of smoke bellying under the low boughs of the pines surrounding his camp. Wen's sleep was shallow, near the surface. Another smell, a distinct meaty odour, began to foul his dreams. *What is that smell?* he wondered. Wen shot out of sleep and saw eyes of liquid fire leaping at him from the dark. Before he could think, he threw himself hard to his right, his arm thrust out. His sudden movement sent the tiger flying past. He could feel its hot breath on his neck. The side of a paw caught his shoulder and knocked him over. As he fell away, the blade of the knife caught and slid across the tiger's throat. Pressing hard, he felt the knife sever the cat's jugular.

Wen scrambled to his feet, panting and rubbing his shoulder. He stared, now wide awake, his heart jumping in his chest. The cat spasmed and quickly died, its blood spurting from its neck into the earth. *I am lucky. A small female.* The knife, razor-sharp, had almost removed the animal's head, it's own falling weight causing the blade to bite deep. Still gripping the knife in his hand, Wen had to use his other hand to loosen his fingers from its hilt.

Sitting near the dead tiger, he watched it all night, until first light awoke the forest. Over the hours, he watched the brilliance drain from its eyes and the vital colour – its yellowish coat, its sharp black stripes – fade subtly. *This is not just an animal,* he thought, *it is a force of nature.* Finally, shouldering his pack, he bent down and placed his hand on the side of the beast, then walked down the trail.

Following a long steady descent through a region of rocky hills and damp forest with no further sign of tigers, he came to a series of farmers' fields where he removed the mulberry-bark mask. Through the morning he passed along a road beside vegetable fields, receiving long stares from the men and women working there in broad-brimmed bamboo hats fastened with ribbons under their chins. They would rise from the deep bows of their labours and stand, watching him until he disappeared. *The way they look at me – what have I become?* he wondered. Eventually, a village loomed in the distance and, as he approached, a few young children gaped at him, skipping off to tell their parents that a stranger – *a ghost from the mountains,* as the children put it – had appeared.

A middle-aged farmer with mud on his hands approached and stopped several yards away, afraid to come too close. He spoke in a language thick with a dialect that Wen was barely able to understand. "Who are you, stranger? What do you want here?"

Several more peasant men gathered nervously from houses nearby. "I come from the South, over the mountains." He turned and looked back. "My master has instructed me to travel to the capital to see the Emperor. I seek food and shelter for a few weeks, before I move on. I can work."

The man had been listening closely with his face distorted, trying to understand. "We seldom see people from over the mountains. How do we know you are not sent by a raiding party of bandits to judge our defences?"

"I am a painter and calligrapher. I know nothing of bandits."

Another peasant, thinner, with one clouded eye, leaned around the bolder man and asked, "What do you carry in your sack?"

"Paintings. Drawings. Some food. My last bit of rice. A cooking pot. Clothing and blankets. I will show you. I have no weapons except this knife in my belt."

Wen released himself from the pack, lowered it into the dust of the road and began to pull out its contents.

A third man, picking his teeth with a stick, stepped forward and said to the others while staring at Wen, "He can come to my house. I need someone to help with grinding grain while I go to the hills to cut wood. Pack up your things and come with me."

The man stood waiting, stocky and rooted to the ground, hemp sandals on his thick dusty feet. Wen packed up his supplies, everyone dispersed and the painter went off with the farmer, whose house was on the far side of the village, next to a wide stream swollen with autumn rains.

As the two men approached the windowless hut, a woman, not old but no longer young, stood in the doorway and waited. When they arrived, she questioned her husband about the stranger, while casting shy sidelong glances at Wen. The husband answered her in gruff tones. They all stepped into the hovel and Wen noticed the woman had a lame leg, which she dragged behind her.

He also noted an old man, toothless, sitting on a pile of hay in one corner of the room.

"My wife can no longer grind grain," the farmer explained, "since she fell and hurt her leg. I have had donkeys that are smarter than this woman." She bowed her head in shame but he ignored her. "And my father here is too old to do any work at all. In two days, I must leave to cut wood with my brothers and their sons in the foothills. You will stay and work. We will feed you well if you work hard. It was a good harvest this year."

Wen nodded. The man indicated a pile of straw on the earth floor in another corner as his bed, so Wen placed his sack there and sat and watched, like the old man across the room, while the woman prepared a meal on the low stove of crumbling brick. The farmer went outside to do a few chores.

A short while later, the food was ready and they all sat on grass mats around the low rough table. Wen felt his body warming and relaxing as he ate the rice porridge mixed with tough autumn greens and a bit of stringy chicken. Throughout the meal, the farmer shovelled the food into his mouth in silence without looking at the woman. She appeared sad and defeated, her head bowed. Wen imagined that she had once been a beautiful girl but the hard years had stolen her beauty away.

A spark of life entered her eyes when, with kindness, she mashed a bowl of food into soft paste for the old man who sat and ate with them, gumming his gruel, but said nothing.

The farmer finished eating and rose from the table. "This afternoon you will help me grind the grain, and tomorrow as well. After that, I will be gone for six or seven days and you must have all the grain finished by my return. Come." He headed for the door, where he kicked a chicken out of his way and went outside. Wen followed.

In a short time, Wen learned all he needed to know about grinding grain. Since the farmer's blind mule had died the previous year, they had to turn the heavy stone themselves by hand. The man showed Wen how to add grain and to push on the heavy wooden pole, smoothed and polished with use, which turned the stone. All day, they walked in a circle, the sweat pouring off them. *I could be halfway to the capital for the distance I have covered today*, thought Wen in late afternoon, but he kept on because he felt that the abundant food he was to receive would be ample payment for the work. When he decided to continue his journey, he figured he could purchase more food from them to take with him. They seemed to have a plentiful supply.

Two days later, the two brothers and their three sons came by in a cart pulled by a bullock. The farmer left with them, warning Wen again that he must have all the grain done by his return. His wife stood watching her husband climb onto the cart, an axe over his shoulder, not giving her a second glance. The woman stared at her husband's broad silent back and the cart disappeared into the distance. Wen noticed that the look she gave her husband in secret was both sad and angry.

For the next several days, Wen applied himself to the work and the woman fed him well, heaping food into his bowl.

On the morning of the third day, a boy appeared in the yard and spoke to the woman. Wen approached. The woman turned to him and said, "The boy says the old man's sister has died, so he must go with this boy to the next village for the funeral rites."

Wen asked, "Will you go?"

"No. I cannot leave the farm while my husband is away."

A short time later, the old man, assisted by the boy, hobbled down the road.

That evening, the woman took out a jug of rice wine and filled two rough grey cups, one of which she offered to him. "Drink," she said.

Seated on the grass mats, they ate and drank. The room was warm as the weather had moderated and the stove had been fired for cooking the meal.

"What is your name?" Wen asked.

She lowered her eyes. "I am called Ling."

"I am Wen."

"The villagers say you are a painter," the woman said, her cheeks flushed from the drink and the warmth.

Wen nodded.

"Will you tell me of your paintings?"

Wen was surprised. "Of course." He looked away to think a moment and when he returned his gaze to her, she was still staring at him, waiting.

He spoke to her for a long while about painting, and showed her the one painting he had finished. She nodded her head when she saw it, smiling, but said nothing. They drank more rice wine from the jug. A light rain and a thick fog had come with the dusk. Wen felt his body sinking and relaxing. It seemed as if his muscles glowed from the arduous work, his head felt thick and his vision blurred pleasantly as the light faded. She lit an oil lamp and placed it on the table and they continued talking and drinking.

"Your husband – he seems an angry and bitter man. Why?"

She lowered her gaze to the table. "I have been unable to give him a son."

After a moment of uncomfortable silence, the woman pointed at the lamp and said, "Look. A good omen."

The wick had opened and spread into the shape of a flower.

"I must sleep," Wen said after a while, rising and moving to his pile of straw in a corner of the room where his pack lay and his blankets were spread. To the glow of the lamp and the patter of rain on the roof, he faded into sleep, barely aware of the woman preparing for bed herself. He noticed she placed several leaves on the stovetop and the room filled with the fragrance of aloes, and then the exhaustion of the day emptied his limbs and he sank into sleep. A moment later, he felt something – the woman slipping under his blanket. "I am cold. Warm me. Please."

He smelled her, the skin of her bare shoulder, and woke with a start. Wen couldn't resist stroking her and soon their two bodies were burning and slick with passion. His hand sliding over her hip felt as it did when he would draw the arc of a distant hill, and when he touched her there, she felt moist and smooth as the tip of his brush engorged with ink. As he made love to her, he looked at her face in the faint lamplight. Years had fallen away. She was young again, eyes glowing, her lips seeking him out. Half the night, they repeatedly gave in to their passions until Wen, utterly exhausted, fell asleep.

The next day, he was unable to grind as much grain as he had the day before. When he went back to the house for the midday meal, he noticed that the woman no longer appeared young but once again looked her age, her face careworn and tired.

That night, she came to his bed again, and again the years fell away from her face as their passion grew. Her face lost twenty years in a few delirious moments of lovemaking.

The next day, Wen was able to grind even less grain than he had done on the first days and again, the woman's face looked lined with age.

For several more days, the pattern continued. Each night, she would lose years in his bed and become a girl again, with skin slippery and smooth as white jade, eyes glowing, and each day he ground less and less grain. He realized he would be able to grind little more than half the grain before the farmer's return but the woman continued her visits. She was both irresistible and insatiable, keeping him awake each night until nearly dawn.

In the middle of the sixth night, Wen, feeling Ling's naked body nestled comfortably next to his, heard a faint sound and opened his eyes. In the dimness, he caught a glint of light. Instantly, he rolled aside. The falling axe cut through the straw of his bed and stuck in the ground. Ling leapt up and screamed. Wen raised himself to his hands and knees. He smelled the heavy odour of rice wine in the air. The farmer, drunk, had tumbled over after his first wild swing of the axe. Wen shouted. The farmer grunted, trying to raise himself up. Ling grabbed the axe and screamed again as her husband bit her hand. Wen leapt upon the farmer's back. A tangle of limbs thrashed in the faint light. Both men shouted. Ling cried out.

A moment later, it was over. In the sudden calm, Wen and Ling panted, and she shook uncontrollably. She tried to cover her nakedness with her hands. The farmer lay on the floor with the axe stuck deep in his forehead, his eyes wide open with surprise. Ling, standing above and staring at him, looked at her palms, and back to her husband. Wen was startled at the strength with which she had wielded the axe. The farmer tried to rise, flopped back down, coughed up a thick gout of blood and died.

Before dawn, they removed the axe from his head and burned the hut with the farmer still in it. Ling would return to her family in a neighbouring village, explaining that her husband was too drunk to escape the fire, and Wen would continue his journey.

By first light, Wen was already several villages away, his pack heavy with new provisions.

[Winter]

Burning Tip

DARK HAS FALLEN. The museum is abandoned. The curator of Chinese art climbs the trails alone, passes through resin-scented forests and explores the mountains of Li Wen. Finally, he stretches, removes the viewing goggles, stands and goes to the window.

His third-floor office overlooks a park. In every direction, the lights of highrises sparkle over the city. A full moon hangs suspended, resembling an artist's stamp impressed on the black heavens. The Chinese picture a white hare in the moon mixing the elixir of immorality. Westerners simply see the face of a man.

For the curator, the moon resembles the pupil of an eye through which he can view mountains and rivers, mountains and rivers without end.

Later, that same night, seated before the painting of winter, he remarks to himself that Wen has used brushstrokes in the unfrozen lake that resemble an oar rippling through water; high in the evergreen trees, the strokes unfold as fans of pine needles; in the sky, they resemble the wind unravelling clouds, while in the highest peaks, the strokes are firm as rock.

The curator now finds the figure of a snow-rimed man walking the whitened winter trail high above the long meandering lake, a brush sticking up from the side of his pack. He follows. He walks in Li Wen's footsteps, and he feels his mind captured by the silence of that place. The silence of the painting enters him and calms the waves in the unfrozen lake, quieting them so thoroughly that a mountain can reflect there in the still waters, a mountain so pure it looks real, though it is made of nothing but light.

∼

After travelling for ten days in the broad valley and passing through dozens of farming villages, Wen arrived at a series of hills that rose next to a long, multi-fingered lake. The views from the ridges above the lake proved magnificent for their clarity – he could see a few fishing boats far below on the water, like simple diagonal *pie* and *na* strokes. He spent half a sunny cool day sketching the lake, the skiffs and the shoreline below, as well as a bitter-cork tree that caught his attention.

Climbing through the forest, he thought, *Now that all the leaves have fallen, each curve, ripple and hill in the landscape is revealed. The forest is as beautiful as a nude woman.*

Late that day he was met by three traders with four laden donkeys coming down from the pass. By speaking with these grinning men, he learned that the town he hoped to reach before winter, Jinhan, was on a plain about ten or twelve days' walk beyond Stone Goddess Mountain, which he was presently ascending. He inquired if the town would be a good place for him to put up for the coldest months. They told him that Jinhan had numerous inns for lodging, places in which they themselves had often stayed. They also mentioned that White Bone Pass remained clear of snow when they had crossed three days before.

"I have walked these trails since I was a boy. The luck of the gods is with you," said Yu, the oldest trader, his sad, heavy-lidded eyes staring at Wen. "Usually, by this time, deep snows have already come to the pass. To be caught in a storm there is death. The bones of my uncle, my mother's brother, are somewhere on that mountain."

The youngest of the traders, named Hui, brought the subject back to Jinhan. He suggested that on arrival in the town, Wen should try the fine rice wine, flavoured with magnolias and pepper, for which Jinhan was famous, as well as the brothels, which housed some of the comeliest women these rough traders had ever seen.

The traders went on talking so long about the girls in the brothels and their arcane knowledge of what would pleasure men, that dark slipped down unnoticed and they decided to camp right where they were, tethering their donkeys to a nearby tree. They asked Wen to join them for a meal, which he was happy to do. Long into the night, Hui recounted his many amorous adventures with a brothel-girl named Ping. Hui said he was going to return to the town and bring her to his village as his wife. The two other traders, older, heavier and stuffed with meat porridge, grunted, having heard it all before.

Mention of the brothel girl brought the memory of the farm woman to Wen's mind. *There was no shame in what happened*, he thought. *She was unhappy, and suffering.* He realized that every time he would pick up his brush to paint a distant mountain, he would feel his hand stroking the curve of her hip, every time he put the brush tip in his mouth to soften it, he would taste her. *I could have stayed with that woman for the rest of my days, but it was impossible. I am fated to deliver the message to the Emperor and, in any case, my presence would have raised too many questions over the death of the farmer. I am sorry he died for he too was suffering.* A pang of regret entered his heart. *The world is woven of joy and sorrow, of delight at what is possible and sadness at what cannot be.*

The traders fell asleep around the fire long before Hui stopped taking advantage of Wen's willing ear. Eventually, Wen realized he had been sound asleep, appearing to listen to Hui's babbling, his plans, his hopes for the future, how wealthy he would be, how this would make Ping love him. His talk kept feeding Wen's regret and sorrow, and his mood darkened. Finally, Wen lay down. Hui kept talking. Then Hui too lay down, and never ceased his blather. Wen awoke in the middle of the night, as was his custom, and heard mumbling. It was Hui talking in his sleep. Wen began to look forward to the silence of his trek over the mountain pass.

In the morning, after rice, a few vegetables and tea, Wen bade farewell to the traders who were packing their donkeys for the trip downhill. Hui waved and shouted to Wen: "When you arrive in Jinhan, tell Ping I will soon return to her a wealthy man." The other two traders guffawed and shook their heads.

Old Yu said, "Like the wind in poplar leaves at the foot of South Mountain, he never stops blowing."

Over the next several days, Wen passed through a region softened by a light snowfall. Although the snow barely came to his ankles, it outlined the trees and smoothed the stony crags of the mountains around him. He stopped often to sketch, breathing on his fingers to warm them. Eventually, from a greater height, he again sighted the lake in the distance below, now banked and surrounded by a blanket of snow, its islands white dots, its surrounding forests a visual feast of light and shadow. This too he drew, adding sheet after sheet to his collection for the winter painting.

As he squatted and sketched, a light breeze silently tumbled snow from the branches of a tall straight pine. The scene reminded him of his hometown in the spring, when the warm breeze would free clouds of white flower petals and mists of pollen from the limbs of peach trees. For the first time since he had started his journey, he felt a sudden pang of homesickness. He thought of his deceased parents, his few friends, Master Wei, the farm woman. He felt a weight on his heart. Sighing, he listened. Not a sound was to be heard for ten thousand *li*.

The trees were thinning and the way was steep. He decided to gather a handful of sticks for his journey over the pass. He stashed them at the top of his pack. *I'm sure a fire will be useful at some point*, he thought. The temperature had dropped considerably the night before and as he hiked up the slope in late morning, the stunted trees and rhododendron bushes disappeared entirely. The world here was made of nothing but bare rock and unreachable boneless silk-grey sky. Slowly, the wind began to pick up and snow started blowing in his face. Stacks of stones every hundred yards marked the trail. He hoped to be over the pass and into the protection of the forest on the other side by nightfall, if all went well.

Starting to hurry, he trudged through the white field, keeping an eye out for the next stone marker. The wind kept building, twisting wildly, swirling snow. The cold penetrated to his bones, through the many layers he had donned in the first light of the frigid morning. He noticed that the wind on this mountain did not whistle or shriek. It blew hard, the snow stung his face, but everything unfolded in a pure, inexpressible silence, like a blank page before the first drop of ink.

He felt he was making good time. The snow was piling up steadily as he hiked from marker to marker. The ancients who had built them made each successive marker a little higher as the mountain rose, to account for the deeper snows. Wen was walking through snow above his knees now, but it was light and powdery and he kept pounding his way forward and upward.

Suddenly his footing gave way beneath him and he slid down a slope next to the trail. One moment he was standing upright, the next he was slipping down the mountain, tumbling through drifts. When his abrupt descent came to its end, he wiped the icy particles from his face, adjusted his pack, and gazed up. He decided he could find his way back to the trail by following the path that he had made through the snow when he fell. On hands and knees he started scrambling up the slope. *It's not far, I did not fall far.*

It took longer than he expected. The steep slope slowed him and the snow and wind had redoubled in ferocity since his tumble. Eventually he regained the trail, or what he thought was the trail. Everywhere he looked – white. Except for... *yes, there it was, the pile of sticks*, right where he had first tumbled over, sitting jumbled on top of the snow. He stared at them – they had fallen in a heap that resembled the strokes of the character for 'struggle'. Gathering them up in a single swipe, he stuffed them back into his sack and tried not to think about the cold now creeping from his feet and up his legs, despite the good animal-skin boots the woman had given him before they had set fire to the hut. *What I wouldn't give for a fire now,* he thought. He was starting to shiver, his teeth chattering uncontrollably. His stomach felt empty, the rice from breakfast having long disappeared. *Perhaps it is later than I realize.*

Now that he was back on the trail, he searched through the storm swirling around him for the next stone marker. There was no sign of it. He looked back the way he had come. The previous markers too had disappeared. He realized the snow was now nearly to his waist. He couldn't see more than ten feet in any direction. The wind drove the snow in a fury.

If I could find an overhang of rock, I could start a fire. With this hope driving him on, he forced his way through the blizzard. After a while, the labour of walking had him sweating underneath his clothes and yet he was still freezing cold. He wrapped a cloth around his head and across his face. Only his eyes were visible. He trudged through swirling arabesques of white dancing wind.

Tucking his head down, he forced himself through the drifts, peering out often, seeking a marker, an overhang of stone, a rock wall of some kind that he could use as protection, but he found nothing.

He worked his way further up the pass. He must have been walking a long while, for he glanced up and saw that the light had weakened. *Dark is coming on.* He hadn't seen a stone marker since he fell. He stopped and turned around. *Should I go back? Impossible.* The snow was now so deep, the air so swirling with white dervishes, that he wasn't sure what was up the mountain and what was down. His own steps from moments before disappeared before his eyes.

Could I burrow under the snow for protection? he wondered. *I would suffocate, I would freeze to death.* He saw a snow lion leaping at him and ducked, but it was only more wind, more snow. *I am so tired. If I could only rest. Just a moment.* He fought against these thoughts and struggled on. The cold worked its way right through into his heart. Even his blood felt icy under his skin. He forced himself to push ahead until the dark came on, and then he walked further still into the blackness, not knowing where he was headed but determined to keep moving. The wind-blown snow never relented for a moment. *And such overwhelming silence. I would even welcome the roar of a tiger at this point. Any sound at all...*

The temptation to rest, to sleep in the soft bed of the snow was irresistible. He fought it and stumbled ahead, but the snow was now so deep that he was struggling just to walk and had to lift his legs high with each step. The wind still raging around him, he tried to clear himself a pocket in the snow, then fell forward. *I must sleep*, he thought, *I must....* At the last moment, he felt the warmth of the woman's body next to him in the straw, flames licking up from the hut.

~

Wen reached out in his half-sleep to touch the stone before his eyes. But it was too distant. Awake now, he smelled smoke. *Where am I?* His body was warm and he realized he was lying under a heavy animal skin that reeked of old dried meat. Glancing about, he saw the back of a bald man leaning over a small table. A fire with a weak flame barely lit the room, sending shadows scurrying haphazardly about the rough stone walls. He raised his head. *Not a room, but a cave.*

On hearing Wen awaken, the man rose stiffly from his stone bench and shuffled over to him. The shaved head and maroon robes revealed that he was a monk. He looked at Wen and smiled a wide, warm smile, but said nothing.

"What happened? Where am I?" Wen asked but the old monk simply continued to smile. "Can you not speak?" The monk responded by indicating that he was indeed incapable of speech. *Or perhaps*, Wen wondered, *he chooses not to speak; perhaps he holds a vow of silence.*

With hand gestures and a few words scratched on a wooden board with a piece of charcoal, the monk was able to communicate to Wen that he had found him half-dead in the snow and had brought him back to his cave. *Yinshi*, he etched the character for hermit on the board, and pointed to himself. He then added the character *héshàng*, or monk. Wen indicated that he understood.

The old man pointed to his mouth while looking at Wen with a question in his eyes.

"Eat? Yes, yes, I'm very hungry," Wen said.

The monk trundled over to the fire and lifted the iron lid from a cauldron, scooped out a bowl of soup for Wen and returned. Wen sat up, took it carefully in his two hands and tilted the bowl to his mouth. He felt the warmth run down his gullet and into his belly in a soothing stream. After Wen had eaten rice, the monk made tea from Wen's own supply.

Wen's pack stood against the stone wall near the foot of his bed of straw. After eating, he inspected the pack, and found that the bamboo brush with the message for the Emperor was untouched. He checked the finished painting of autumn, his other brushes and, somewhat covertly and with a touch of guilt, the money strings and other valuables. Everything was in perfect order. Only the tea had been removed.

The old monk too had eaten, then returned to his seat by the table. He stared down at the page of a manuscript laid out before him. The light in the cave was dim from the few dying coals remaining in the fire, the meagre smoke disappearing into fissures high in the ragged ceiling of the cave. Near the fire was stacked a pile of sticks and a few flattened chunks of dried animal dung.

After inspecting his pack, Wen approached the monk who turned and glanced at him but did not seem to mind that his visitor wished to see what he was reading. Wen looked over the hermit's shoulder. As the monk leaned over the long rectangular manuscript, he held a lit stick of incense and in the near darkness he breathed on its burning tip. By the faint light, the monk could read a few lines on the page and contemplate them. Wen read from what he recognized as *The Diamond Sutra* of the Buddha: *Great Ones, perfect beyond learning, utter no words of teaching. The truth is uncontainable and inexpressible. It neither is nor is not.* That was the limit of what Wen could see before the pulsation of light from the stick of incense faded. The monk had closed his eyes and Wen realized he was contemplating the words.

Wen returned to his bed of straw and, for the first time, noticed the uncanny silence in this place. It was a silence filled with space and luminosity. Wen saw through the gloom that a heavy blanket covered what he took to be the entrance to the cave about fifteen steps away. He edged through the dark to the cave mouth and pulled the blanket back, revealing a world of pure snow under a sliver of moon nearly riding on its back. The black sky was dusted with diamonds.

Over the next few days, Wen recovered his strength. He learned that it would be impossible for him to reach the town of Jinhan on the far side of the mountain because of the snow, which piled up higher and higher day after day. When Wen asked what he should do, the monk shrugged and wrote the character for 'spring' on his board. Wen stared at the word a moment and then nodded to the monk, resigning himself to a long stay. He took the small amount of food in his pack and added it to the hermit's supplies, which were simple but considerable. He glanced about the cave. *At least it is reasonably warm, there seems to be enough rice and tea to get us both through the winter and I won't have to worry about the old monk demanding my attention with useless talk.*

In fact, the monk spent most of his time in his meditations and his studies. For the most part, he ignored Wen's presence. But he proved generous with his food and seemed to enjoy Wen's gift of tea immensely, breaking into a huge smile after each sip.

The cave proved spacious enough for the two men to disappear from each other's sight, with several twisting paths that wound deep into the mountain. Using a torch from the fire to light his way, Wen explored these paths and found smaller caves, more tunnels, and a pool that the monk used as a source of fresh water.

On sunny days, the monk removed the blanket from the entrance and light flooded deep into the cavern. If it wasn't windy, the sunlight reflecting off the snow brought a modicum of warmth with it.

Wen would sit in the cave mouth and soak up the sunlight, letting its rays warm his face.

After a week of rest and exploring the cave, Wen began to join the monk in his morning meditations. The hermit appeared unaffected by this, neither encouraging nor discouraging it. He accepted it as he seemed to accept everything else.

At the cave entrance, an overhanging rock ledge kept a wide, flat area relatively free of snow and it was here that Wen, one sunny morning, set out the materials to begin his next painting. From his pack, he retrieved the numerous sketches that he had done lower down the mountain, unrolling them from their bamboo tube. After a thorough investigation of these drawings, he selected the brushes, which he placed in a pot of warm water from the fire, and set out an ink stick and the turtleshell inkstone. He unrolled a piece of blank paper and weighed it down at the corners and sides with stones. Another small flat stone he used as a brush rest.

The monk wandered down from his meditations to see what Wen was doing. He glanced at the brushes, the ink stick and inkstone, as well as the paper – took it all in, and promptly returned to his semi-darkness deeper in the cave.

As Wen began to grind his ink in the turtle shell, his mind drifted to memories of his first calligraphy and painting lessons with his master, Fu Wei. Wei had been known as a highly disciplined teacher. His teaching was the way of iron, not the way of water. After spending a year working on nothing other than developing his skill in calligraphy, Wen was finally allowed to proceed to painting. Wen, who was clearly a slow learner and stiff with resistance, was told to paint the image of a mustard seed over and over as practice, as if he were a child. *Why am I painting this ridiculous mustard seed?* he had asked himself. *All mustard seeds look exactly the same.* He would pick up his brush, place his fingers in the prescribed manner, and paint the same tiny seed again and again. *Why am I painting this stupid mustard seed?* As his drive to discipline himself met the granite wall of his resistance, the words rang out louder in his head: *Why am I painting this mustard seed?*

Each time he finished, his master would approach and look at the drawing. Sometimes he simply shook his head, as if Wen were an idiot and incapable of learning anything. The Master explained. "The mustard seed is a single dot, the *dian* stroke. That is all. A dot – no more. Simplify yourself." After the thirtieth painting, he had said, "A waste of paper." Next time, he had added, "A waste of ink, too." Wen was fuming. In his anger, he dashed something off. This time, when One Tooth came to look, before he dismissed it there was the slightest, almost imperceptible, pause. Wen had noticed, and had taken heart.

After sixty paintings, the mustard seed, which at first had looked exactly like all other mustard seeds, had begun to take on its own unique characteristics. It was not as smooth as it had seemed at first. It revealed contours, edges, textures; it wasn't perfectly round for it had a tiny flat spot on one side, a detail that had gone unnoticed previously. Its colour was no longer dull but opulent, taking on a richness and depth in Wen's eyes. By the hundredth painting it glowed gold and Wen had begun to feel a genuine sympathy for this lowly mustard seed. He could feel it longing for the sun, longing to burst from its vegetal shell and extend its slim green limbs into the light.

After hundreds of paintings over several weeks, he had begun to feel that he could paint the mustard seed forever. It was a delight to feel the brush soak up ink and swirl onto the paper, the mustard seed appearing out of nowhere. Just a dot, a single dot, accomplished with a single motion.

One time, when he went to pick up the brush he heard the voice of his father. 'Hold the brush in the same way I taught you to hold the pole on the river – with attention. Not too tight and not too loose. Even though your left hand appears empty, it is full of emptiness. Hold this emptiness in balance with the brush.'

It was then that Wen realized that every true stroke he made would honour his father, and every poor, thoughtless or lazy stroke would bring shame upon himself and his ancestors.

Master Wei stood before him. "Stop," he said. "That is enough. Come with me." He had walked the young man outside and pointed to a stalk of bamboo that was no more than five feet tall. "Now do the same with this bamboo. Start with a single stroke. You must learn how to accomplish a single stroke. And then another. And another. You must become the bamboo, the segments of its stalk and its pointed leaves, its unique shade of green. Brilliance is always utterly simple."

Wen wanted to go back to the mustard seed, but he had to let it go and learn all over again, from the beginning, as if he were an infant learning a new language, one word at a time. One word alone, he had discovered, was not a language. A single dot was not a painting. But that was all long ago.

Wen continued grinding the stick in the cave mouth. He sat on a stone overlooking the blank page, thinking about the next work that he would paint for the Emperor – the winter landscape.

He stopped grinding and gazed out. The snow was absolutely pure, the sky such a deep blue it appeared wet as pigment, the sunlight a luminous yellow. *I have never before been so relaxed and at my ease. At peace utterly. I could stay here, in this cave, forever. Drop all the annoyances of the world and just be at peace, right here, wanting nothing, seeking nothing.*

At that moment, the bamboo in which he carried the message for the Emperor flashed into his mind. *Ah, but I forget. I have my duty to fulfill. To stay here would bring me great joy but I must continue on when spring arrives. I cannot stay. I must deliver the message as well as the paintings. I have promised.*

Sighing with a sense of resignation, he turned to his sketches. He recalled the scenes of the mountainside under snow, rocks and cliffs softened, the branches of the pines and maples, cypress and catalpa outlined in white, the long meandering lake black and arcing and stretching far below, the fishermens' boats, the islands in the distance. One boat was dominated by a towering cliff underneath which it was moored. An ancient overhanging lacebark pine tree jutted out from above. This was one image he knew he would include in the final painting. He realized he could take his time with the painting – he had the remainder of the winter to accomplish it.

The painting began to flicker within him, not just images, but the vital quality that would make it breathe. Its first whisper was like a breeze rippling the still water of a lake. By taking his time, he would imbue the painted landscape with the peace and calm of a winter spent in this cave in the mountains. The quiet that was entering him from the mountain below would pass through him into the mountains in the painting.

Without hurry, he ground the ink, his left hand cupped and holding the turtle shell as he gripped the stick with the right and scraped and swirled it against the shell's inner surface. The black ink pooled and he began to consider his first stroke. Before that stroke, everything was chaos, ink was simply ink, brush was brush, paper was paper, mountain mountain, snow snow. They were disparate fragments of the world, without harmony.

The first touch of brush on paper would start to resolve the chaos, a pulse driving the stroke right out to its tip. His hand would know where to move, and the painting would take on the life of the mountain as it passed through him.

Kneeling before the blank page, he held the brush of silk strands. He took care to grip its handle with precision, placing his fingers as he had been taught – the slim bamboo nestled between the thumb on one side and his index and middle fingers on the other, the remaining two fingers supporting from below. His grip on the brush was firm but not too tight, leaving a space between palm and fingers.

The ink had pooled, the paper was achingly pure and unsullied, the brush about to leap into life. He waited, staring, the blank sheet like an untouched field of snow. Holding the silk strand brush, he waited and waited and finally the painting began to rise from the page, as if it were a landscape appearing in a mirror, or the reflection of a mountain appearing on the surface of a lake as the waters settle. He set down the silk strand brush, which had never touched ink, and picked up the horsehair brush, dipping its point in liquid night.

The first stroke would be no accident but would arrive on the page direct, without hesitation, an arrow of light falling from a star. And so it began – with a single stroke.

Throughout the rest of the winter he worked on the painting and, with time, it took on the silence of falling snow.

∼

One day, as Li Wen worked in the sunlit entrance to the cave, he noticed that the ink ran more freely than it had in a long while. For weeks before, during the colder weather, the ink had felt stiff and unyielding, and his work had taken on a hard and rigid feel. But now, his brush again flowed down the page, the ink splashed and played down the mountain under a swelling sun.

By the time Wen finished the painting a few days later, the world of white outside the cave was melting away. As the days passed, the sun's power swelled, the snow sank lower, birds arrived to peck between the rocks around the cave mouth. Wen brushed a winter poem onto the landscape one afternoon and the next morning he applied his artist's seal to it.

> *Under the snow*
> *the mountain freezes hard*
>
> *No leaves shiver no birds call*
> *the moon lights the world in silence*
>
> *Because winter is dark and long*
> *the snow glows soft and brilliant*
> *Sad on leaving an old friend*
> *yet what joy – walking mountain paths alone*

* * *

Outside, the white world was rushing away to oblivion. In the painting, the heavy snow weighing on the horizontal branches of pine did not melt. The snow on those branches would outlast the next seven hundred springs.

Wen felt silence rise out of the winter painting as heat rises out of the earth itself. From the cave mouth, Wen gazed out on the world. It was time to move on.

The monk sensed something had changed. He came down into the light where Wen's painting was spread on the flat ground. His rheumy old eyes stared at it without giving away anything as to how he felt about the painting. When he noticed the willow tree in the painting by the snow-driven lake far below the mountain, he knew it was a sign that his unexpected visitor would soon be leaving.

The monk glanced out of the cave at the dissolving world and the burgeoning spring without reaction or response. Pulling his robes closer around him, he returned to the cave and his meditations.

Several days later, when the painting had dried thoroughly, Wen added it to the autumn painting and rolled the two together into the bamboo tube. He packed up his materials and just enough rice for his journey down to the city on the plain and left the small amount of remaining tea with the grateful monk.

Shouldering his pack in the bright morning light at the cave entrance, Wen was anxious to move, to stretch his legs, to feel the pull of weight on his shoulders, to exercise his neglected body. He bowed to the monk who bowed back. Wen turned away and edged out into the calf high snow that remained, heading down the mountain to where the Ronghua River would be raging with spring. Once he crossed the river, he planned to hike across the long plain to the city of Jinhan.

Before heading down the trail, he turned and looked back towards the monk who had disappeared from the cave entrance. Then Wen gazed back in the direction he had come months earlier. Standing near the highest point of the mountain, he could see the panoramic view in all directions. A spark of joy – a feeling of lightheartedness and buoyancy – flashed through him, and he thought, *I would do it all again.*

[Spring]

Iron Bell

THE CURATOR OF CHINESE ART turns from Li Wen's painting of winter, goes to his window and gazes out on the park. He notes that the contourless, washed-out clouds of the sky above the city are in a style of painting that Chinese artists call 'boneless.'

The winter, with its silent midnight snows and spitting sleet, its numbing cold and sudden messy thaws, its culling of the elderly and its frost art on glass – winter in all its cruel beauty, loveliness and pain, is finally coming to an end. When one is inside it, it feels endless. But once over, it seems to have passed – *now autumn, now winter, now spring* – as quickly as words in a sentence.

When he returns to his chair, he finds himself seated before the painting of spring. He sees a frieze of mountains angling into the distance and realizes the artist is able to see the landscape from a bird's eye view, can picture the mountain from all sides at once, from all angles.

Later, that same night, the curator is visited by a dream. He climbs a mountain trail, working hard, passing through pine forests mottled with silver moonlight, a luminescent dust floating in the air under the branches. Eventually the trail breaks into an open space ringed with maple and oak trees. Under one of the oaks, its upper branches festooned with constellations, he notices a Chinese man asleep. Wondering, the curator stares at the sleeping man – *perhaps this is not my dream but Li Wen's.*

To the west, mountains stretch into the distance. A wind comes up and he sees the landscape waver with the breeze like a painting hanging from a tree branch. The wind continues to circle, flowing around the glade, and he discovers that each of the four directions holds a painting, one for each season.

When the breeze dies, the paintings grow still and dissolve back into the landscape.

~

It seemed the entire world was melting away, as if the mountains themselves were turning liquid and flowing down into the valleys. Water dripped and streamed from overhanging rocks, and sluiced into gathering rivulets. Water fell in cascading waterfalls like chrysanthemums tumbling. In places, the trail itself ran ankle-deep in water. The world was all change.

Occasionally, through the evergreens, he caught glimpses of the Ronghua River and he wondered how he would cross in this season of rushing floods.

Two days later, approaching the river along a soggy, rutted road, he came upon a ferry loading with passengers. The ferry teemed with traders and merchants, farmers with baskets on their backs, peasants tugging donkeys and carrying chickens. A cart pulled up and four men jumped down to unload a wooden coffin. The crowd parted and watched the men haul the coffin onto the ferry. A long line of mourners followed. Wen joined in behind and paid the ferryman as he boarded.

"Our father's native village is on the far side of the river," Wen overheard one of the coffin-bearers reply to a question from a passenger. "We must take our poor father across and bury him there with his ancestors."

While pushing his way to the other side of the ferry, Wen noted the turbulent greyish-brown waves of the fast-rushing river. Having been a ferryman himself, albeit on a much smaller boat, he had some experience of rivers, and he didn't like what he saw. Here the roar of the water overwhelmed the excited gabbling of the peasants. A heavy towrope ran from the ferry across the river to the other shore. It wasn't a wide river at this point so Wen could easily make out the two bullocks and the line of half-naked boat-towers on the far side who would haul on the hawser to pull the ferry across. Shouldering his way out of his pack, Wen placed the bag at his feet, tucking it under the bulwark at the side of the boat, and prepared for the crossing.

Halfway across, it was clear the ferry was in trouble. The power of the river's current had tugged one roped bullock into the water where it was panicking and no longer able to pull. Peasants on board were pointing and Wen could see the wide-open mouth of the wailing animal as it fought against drowning. The remaining bullock and the crowd of men straining on the rope were unable to control the boat and it began to slip downriver.

When it became clear to the passengers that something was going wrong on the far shore, they rushed in a crowd to one side of the ferry to see, causing the boat to tip, tossing three-quarters of the passengers, including Wen, into the churning water. Once it lost its load, the ferry straightened and continued to rush downriver.

Wen found himself in the icy waves. He tried to swim toward shore but was forced swiftly downstream, taking in gulps of air mixed with water. All around, drowning passengers and animals thrashed and screamed and clutched at him. He received a glancing blow in the side from a terrified donkey kicking wildly in the water, and lost his breath. The water swirled and rolled, tumultuous waves crashing on his head and streaking by.

The lid of the coffin swished past him, followed by the corpse. He tried to fight against the current but kept going under and swallowing water. He was swept downriver and again went under, choking and flailing. A wave passed and his head popped out of the water. He spotted the coffin itself bearing down on him. In one quick motion he pulled himself up and flipped into the coffin where he landed hard on his back, coughing and gagging, and passed out.

Wen awoke and gazed up into pure blue. He realized he was still inside the coffin. All was quiet. He sat up and looked about and discovered that the coffin was partially beached on a sandy bay, which was connected by a narrow channel to the river. He shook his head, touched the ache in his side. *I remember...a donkey kicked me.* He shook his head again, trying to clear the mist behind his eyes. *My pack!* He swivelled about and spotted the ferry, caught on a sandbar. Climbing from the coffin, he ran around the bay, stumbling in the shallow water. Approaching the ferry, he saw small clusters of people standing and weeping over the bodies of drowned passengers. The corpses had washed up on shore.

He came upon a woman sitting in the shallows holding a little girl in her arms. The mother was rocking back and forth and wailing. Nearby a man was squatting and staring silently at the ground. Forgetting about his pack for a moment, Wen stopped and looked at them. Then he heard more wailing from other parts of the bay and noticed other bodies. When he saw a young man holding an older man with straggly grey hair, it reminded him of his own father, who had drowned years before. The body of his father had never been found, though a farmer on shore told Wen he had seen him tumble in from his boat. *There seemed no reason for it*, the farmer had said. *One moment he appeared to be staring at his reflection, the next moment, he was in the water. It seemed that he wanted to fall.* Wen pictured his father, who had spent a lifetime going back and forth across the water, as part of the river now, a ripple in the current, flowing on and on forever.

Wen walked a distance from the others, sank down into the sand, put his head on his knees and wept.

After a while, Wen stood and waded out to the ferry through a stand of tall reeds. He felt like he had a stone in his chest and his feet dragged. Several men stood in the shallow water trying to assess how best to pull the ferry off the sandbar, while a dozen passengers stood on shore watching and offering suggestions. Wen found a rope ladder hanging down the ferry's side and climbed aboard. He saw the pack immediately. It had been caught up under the bulwark, and was still dry. Shrugging it on, he climbed down, asked directions for the town of Jinhan and, with bowed head and slumped shoulders, trudged on.

After eight days of walking through dull, dusty countryside that became progressively drier, Wen entered the town of Jinhan. The evening horns were sounding as the guards pulled the gates shut behind him. Everyone outside hurried to get in, scurrying and shouting, driving their donkeys and draft animals ahead of them. A few riders in the distance spurred their horses on and galloped through just in time. Along with them came a dozen dust-covered farm labourers – hoes atop shoulders – who had been working in the fields to prepare the soil for planting. Spring was further advanced down here in the valley than it had been on the slopes of the mountains.

Wen asked one of the farm workers who was walking next to him, a sturdy young man in loose-hanging, threadbare clothes: "Why is everyone hurrying to get into the town?"

"Where have you come from?" the farmer stopped and looked at Wen as if just noticing him among the crowd of people that had pushed through into the street leading from the gate.

"From over the mountains, and before that, from the far south."

The young man looked at him blankly. Shaking himself out of his reverie, he said, "There has been a drought for three years in the lands beyond Jinhan. The wild lands are filled with bandits. Many people have starved. The farms are dry and the landlords who have rice in storage have kept their supplies hidden so they can drive up the price. The drought has only just started around Jinhan. We still have some water coming down from the distant hills. So, the bandits come to steal our food and … for other purposes."

The peasant looked around. It seemed he wanted to join his friends marching off into the town. "Come," he waved to Wen to follow him.

"Wait," Wen said, "what do you mean – other purposes?"

The peasant didn't answer but was intent on joining his friends.

Wen noticed an inn and had an idea. "Come, drink with me at the tavern, and eat. I will pay." The young man was astonished that someone who looked as poor as himself could afford to pay for another to eat and drink with him.

Down the rutted street, they saw the lank banner marking the location of the tavern. As they entered, the innkeeper looked up and stared at the peasant in dusty clothes and the odd-looking stranger. He frowned, thinking they would be unable to pay. Wen approached an empty table and sat down without hesitation, while the young peasant cringed behind him and took a seat. Wen watched as the peasant bowed his head, his wary eyes seeming to take in everything around him: the wealthy men at other tables and the sight of fine food and drink. The delicious smell of roasted pork hung in the air.

The proprietor strode up to them. "You can't have that in here." He pointed to the hoe. The young farmer clutched it tighter. "Do not worry, young peasant. I'll give it back when you leave. Look, the others have left their swords, have they not?" He turned and pointed at the wall beside the entrance where a number of short swords were piled on a shelf. "You have nothing to worry about. You'll get your precious hoe back."

Several men at other tables laughed at this. The farmer looked at Wen as if asking what he should do. "Do as he says," suggested Wen, and asked the innkeeper, "Shall I place my sack over there as well." The proprietor, who was nearly bald with a long bump on his forehead above the eyes, shook his head. "Not necessary."

"Wine for us. And something to eat," Wen said.

"We have rice and pork. Three copper coins each."

Wen had coins ready in his pocket and slapped them onto the table. The young peasant stared in astonishment, but before he could close his mouth, the innkeeper had whisked the coins into his hand and gone off to retrieve the food and drink.

A few minutes later, he returned with two bowls of rice and meat. He plopped these down on the table, and went to ladle two cups of rice wine from an open iron pot on legs at the far end of the room.

Wen and the peasant drank and ate quickly and in silence. They were both hungry and the wine further sparked their appetites.

Halfway through his bowl of rice, Wen paused and sighed. "So, you were going to tell me more about the bandits in the wild lands beyond Jinhan. What is your name, by the way? I am Li Wen."

The peasant wiped his mouth on the back of his hand. He took a slug of wine and licked his lips. "I am called Xu Ming. They say the wild people in those lands are making sacrifices to try to bring back the rains, human sacrifices to end the drought." He hadn't said a thing since entering the inn and now the words rushed out in a torrent. "They butcher our townspeople and our farmers. Old people. Children. Men and women. They killed a girl right outside the gates. I knew her. A farm worker, she fell and hurt her leg running back from the fields and the gates closed. The guards wouldn't let her in because it was already dark and the bandits could rush in if the gates were opened. We heard her screaming out in the fields, but no one would go out to save her. Everyone was afraid. We could hear the horsemen. They always arrive just after dark to grab stragglers. The gate guards say that the sound of the watch drums are drawing hungry tigers down from the hills. Last week, one of the guards who was trying to scare them off was snatched away." He stopped as quickly as he had started and began gobbling his food again, his chopsticks working furiously, bowl raised to just under his mouth.

Wen thought a moment, then said, "I must travel to the capital city, Linan, far to the northeast of here. Is there any way around the dry lands?"

"No." The peasant Ming shook his head. "From Jinhan there are but two directions: back over the mountains or through the wild lands. There is no other way." He took a long draught from his cup of rice wine. "Why do you go to Linan?"

Wen decided it would be best to keep the explanation simple for the young farmer. "My teacher has sent me."

"Ah." This seemed to satisfy him.

"You have enjoyed the food?"

Ming nodded vigorously.

They fell into a comfortable, satiated silence. Then Ming spoke. "You must go to Linan?"

"Yes."

"Because your teacher has sent you?"

"Yes, as I said."

"I will come with you."

"What!?" Wen coughed and spluttered on the last of his rice wine. "You would risk coming with me? Why?"

"You will need protection. I am strong."

"Yes, no doubt you are strong, but against horsemen with swords and knives? What could you do?" Wen smiled. "Defend me with your hoe?" Immediately, Wen regretted having said it.

Ming fell into silence and bowed his head.

Wen hesitated, drumming his fingers on the table. *Perhaps this is a gift from Heaven, this young strong peasant who has so readily offered his help, a gift from the ancestors to help protect me on this difficult part of my journey. Perhaps young Ming has his own reasons for leaving his town. A little companionship could be helpful. If nothing else, he knows when to keep his silence.* Wen leaned forward. "Another cup of wine?"

Two days later, leading a small donkey Wen had bought from a dealer in the town's market, the new friends approached the North gate. Wen stopped to read a placard that was affixed to the wall. Ming, unable to read, stood by waiting while Wen considered the official pronouncement in silence.

Official Order of the Circuit Commissioner
In many villages of this circuit, there are families who kill in order to perform human sacrifices to ghosts. Ordinarily such families send their followers to purchase living persons or seduce and

detain common people. Failing this they use their servants for human sacrifice or as a last resort their own sons or daughters as substitutes. They then slice the corpse and boil or fry it. The ignorance of foolish customs has reached this extreme. The regulations of the Imperial Court explicitly prohibit this practice.

Patrolling military inspectors and district sheriffs will pursue and arrest offenders. District magistrates will give this matter particular attention. Those who trade in living persons in any of the four directions will be arrested. Neighbourhood security forces organized as guard units are charged with the responsibility for reporting on each other's violations. Each report will be rewarded with a payment of three thousand coins.

Violators, whether leaders or followers, will be executed by slicing. Their families will be registered on the penal lists. Family property will be confiscated for use as a fund for paying rewards.

When Wen finished, Ming asked, "What does it say?"

Wen explained. When he mentioned execution by slicing, which was the most feared punishment meted out by the authorities, Ming blanched and his eyes grew wide. "But I hear the military inspectors and district sheriffs have stopped going out to the villages," Ming said. "Like everyone else, they fear leaving Jinhan."

Shouldering their packs, they headed through the open gate into a spring morning. The surrounding fields were covered in a low glowing mist – more dust than moisture – shimmering and shot through with arrows of sunlight.

Ming's pack was filled with rice and vegetables and Wen's with his paintings, brushes and other supplies. The donkey was laden with skins of water and bags of feed and extra rice for there were few wells or pools and little forage in the dry lands ahead.

Ming strode proudly down the path through a field – a curved, two-handed broad sword strapped across the pack on his back. Wen had bought it for him the day before. Ming was wide, large and solid and Wen had watched as, taking the heavy sword from the dealer in the marketplace, he had handled it with ease.

"Let's hope your sword can do more than cut the wind," Wen had commented.

Beside Ming, Wen walked easily, enjoying the feel of his legs swinging and the earth passing beneath his feet. A wide-bladed, single-edged dao sword with a hilt of shark skin hung from his waist on one side, and his long straight knife was tucked into his belt on the other.

∽

Wen and the peasant, Ming, headed northeast, tramping through flat farming country that was increasingly dry and deserted. All day they passed the mummified remains of animals beside the dirt track – donkeys, a few goats, once a bullock. Late in the afternoon, they came upon a dead horse, the ribs of the beast under its dry hide resembling a pair of gnarled hands holding the horse's torso in a death grip.

After the first few days, they saw no one. Most of the farmers had fled the region. There was nothing to eat, little would grow, and wells were choked with dust. As they walked, mute puffs kicked up by their feet settled back onto the trail. At times, it seemed even the wind had abandoned this place. And when a murmur of breeze did arise, it was dry and odourless, drawing what little moisture was left out of the air. The inside of Wen's mouth felt like desiccated leather and he kept it shut to keep his throat from drying out further. More than once, they congratulated themselves for having the foresight to bring the waterskins carried by the little donkey. Nevertheless, what they had brought was barely sufficient.

They would go hours without speaking, marching doggedly on, heads bowed, looking neither left nor right. There was nothing to say and nothing to see; there was only walking to be done – in the distance a bone-white tree to reach, and another day to put behind them. They stopped looking for any farmers or merchants in the abandoned villages they passed. In some cases, the villagers' huts were already caving in, collapsing from neglect. They rationed their supply of water, took bird-sized sips when they stopped to rest, and never rested for long. After four days, their urine came out in meagre, brownish-yellow streams. They were eager to pass beyond this forbidding land and were constantly on the lookout for armed riders.

At night, they would leave the road and find a gully to sleep in, or a pile of stones to lie behind, first checking for snakes. On the fifth night, Wen lay on his back on the hard ground, and stared into the heavens. With the lack of moisture in the air, the stars were sharp as knives. He watched them but a few moments and started to descend into sleep while a full moon, tantalizing as a ripe peach, settled low on the horizon. As he drifted, he heard riders approaching along the road. Opening his eyes and raising himself up on his elbow, he watched a cloud of dust drift through the moonlight. The horses pounded into the distance and disappeared toward Jinhan.

Ming too had awakened. Wen turned to the young farmer stretched out next to him. "Ming, are you sorry you have come?"

There was no hesitation. "No. Already, travelling has entered my blood. I do not think I could live again without moving, even through this blasted landscape, even here." He paused. "When you showed me your paintings in the town, I knew immediately that you are a master although I know nothing of painting. It is an honour to serve a great master. I will help you to reach the Emperor. It is my duty now."

"Because I bought you a meal or two, a few cups of wine, you would do so much for me?"

"There are few things I am good at. I can swing a hoe and now I am learning how to handle a sword. But there is one thing I have always excelled at and that is loyalty. It is all I am good for. You give me the opportunity to exercise the one natural skill I have. To be loyal."

In the morning, they decided not to chance a fire with its highly visible finger of smoke, but simply munched on raw radishes.

They walked on, coming by late morning to an area of low rolling hills, brown and burnt, stripped of vegetation. The track turned a corner to reveal a cart tipped on its side, one if its wheels still slowly turning. Two dead men on the ground beside the cart had been butchered, dark patches staining the sandy soil around their bodies. The stench of blood and death hung in the air. They hurried away from the dirt track to find somewhere to hide, and then saw the horsemen charging.

Riding hard and fast, the dozen bandits drove at them, wailing and shouting, waving their swords wildly in the air. Wen glanced at Ming who stood frozen, his mouth hanging open, unable to draw his great sword. Wen turned back to face the riders. *They are too many.* He realized resistance against such a flurry of swords was useless. "Stand still. Stand your ground," he said to Ming. "Show no fear." Wen steeled himself as the riders approached, their swords like shining reeds stirring in the wind. Just short of Wen and Ming the leader reined in his horse and the band of brigands stopped behind him. The chief bandit, his clothes rags hanging off him, his beard stringy and filthy, leered at them with yellowed eyes. "Throw down your weapons!" he shouted as he halted, holding up his arm with the gleaming curved sword in it. Half turning in his seat, he shouted, "Take their swords! If they resist, butcher them." He tossed a rope to another bandit who had ridden up beside him. "Tie up their hands. We will run them to let them know who rules this desert, but I don't want them dead. I have a use for these two strangers who show so little fear."

The second rider nodded, took the rope, slid down from his horse and tied the hands of Wen and Ming. Other bandits snatched their weapons. "Give me that knife," the leader motioned to one of his men, pointing at the straight knife in Wen's belt. He took it, examined it a moment, ran his thumb along the blade and shoved it behind his own belt.

Wen and Ming were roped to the bandits' horses and the riders started back the way they had come, deeper into the bare rolling hills.

The leader did not run the horses hard and yet it was all Ming and Wen could do to keep up, especially laden with their packs. The leader kept an eye out and when either of them fell, he would stop everyone until Ming or Wen was able to stand again. At one point, he directed one of his men to give them a drink of brackish water from a goatskin. "I want them alive," the leader mumbled. The two prisoners were soon scraped and bruised and covered in dust.

Before arriving at the camp, the band of brigands cut through a narrow defile thick with low dry brush. Here they were forced to ride single file and Wen found himself at the end of the column. While he ran and stumbled along, Wen thought, *I must shed this pack before they examine its contents. This is the place to do it. Now!* Wen fell and this time he was dragged a ways. By rolling over on his back he was able to break the straps and wriggle out of his pack and, while lying on the ground, he quickly kicked it into the bushes. Thinking he was attempting to loosen the rope, the horseman finally turned and shouted, "Stop pulling or I'll have your head!" Because the bandit was the last in line, he worried about keeping pace with the others. "On your feet!" he shouted and was quick to ride on as soon as Wen stood. The rider never noticed the missing pack.

The camp stood at the edge of low hills, near a stinking pool of mud and stagnant water. A cluster of straggly green willows, the only stand of trees within sight, surrounded the pool. Several makeshift huts of bark and branches stood between the trees and the base of a hill. The riders slipped from their horses and let the animals drink from the pool the colour of copper coins. Wen noted that there were three other men, and four women already at the camp. Two of the women had young children in their arms. One of the infants was wailing.

The youngest of the horsemen – a boy of thirteen or fourteen – shouted as he approached the others: "We found a wagon and killed two men, and captured two more. Look," he held up three bulging skins, "wine from the cart!"

"Zhi. Who are these men?" a woman addressed the leader, as Wen and Ming were untied.

Zhi looked his captives up and down. "Prisoners." Wen glanced at Ming whose head was bowed, blood streaming from his lip and forehead.

"We cannot feed ourselves; how will we feed prisoners? For a long while now we have been wasting food on that girl you captured. We must kill them." The woman grabbed a handful of Wen's shirt.

Zhi grasped her upper arm. "No. Listen to me. I have a use for them. We will not keep them long."

Reluctantly, the woman released Wen. "Don't be a fool. We must kill them!"

Zhi pulled the knife from his belt and pointed it at the woman. He said nothing but the action alone was enough to silence her. She turned and ripped the pack off Ming's back and tore it open, pulling out the sacks of food.

Seeing this, Zhi turned to Wen. "Where is your sack? What has happened to it?"

"It fell off when we were running behind the horses."

Zhi turned on the rider who had been pulling Wen, a stocky man with wrinkles carved into his forehead. "You didn't see his sack fall? Hong, answer me."

The man bowed his head. "No. I did not notice."

Zhi slapped him hard in the face, sending Hong reeling. "Truly, I am surrounded by fools!" Grabbing Hong by the shoulder he shoved him to the ground where he knelt, head still bowed. Zhi slid Wen's knife from his belt again, grasped Hong's hair and pulled his head back, exposing his neck with its prominent Adam's apple. But instead of slitting his throat in a single hard stroke, he gently drew the knife across Hong's neck, exposing a fine thread of blood. "Such a knife," he mumbled, smiling, bringing it close to his face and gazing at it. "It leaps into my hand, as if angry." Then he licked it clean of Hong's blood and returned it to his belt. "Get out of my sight," he said to Hong.

* * *

As it was approaching evening, everyone gathered around a fire that held a three-legged iron vessel in which rice cooked, and what smelled to Wen like horsemeat. "Give them bowls and fill them," Zhi ordered the women. "They will need strength for their journey."

As he ate along with the others, Wen wondered what Zhi had meant. When the wine skin was passed, Zhi did not allow Wen and Ming to drink. The others, men and women both, drank greedily, and when the first skin was emptied, Zhi flung it aside and started on another. Four more skins had appeared from the backs of the horses, their haul from the wagon.

The bandits drank fast, trying to ease an unquenchable thirst. "It has been too long since we had wine," Zhi said to his men. "Drink, drink your fill. Tonight we celebrate."

Zhi, his eyes already swimming, ordered two of his men to bring Ming forward. "Show no fear," Wen whispered to Ming. They dragged him away and forced him to kneel before Zhi. Ming gathered his strength and was able to keep from whimpering, but he was glad that one of the thieves rammed a lump of dirty cloth in his mouth when he saw Zhi sliding Wen's knife out from his belt. The cloth would keep him from screaming. "Your left hand," Zhi commanded.

With a few quick deft strokes of the blade, he incised the character for 'messenger' in Ming's palm. The young farmer was astonished at first that it caused no pain, so sharp was the knife. Ming's amazement could be seen in his startled eyes as he stared at his hand. Then the blood gushed and the pain blossomed in his head. Wen heard a roar rumble up Ming's throat and stay there, behind the deeply rammed cloth.

"The other hand," demanded Zhi. Ming was frozen, so the brigand on that side grasped the prisoner's right arm and held it forth. Ming passed out. Again, holding the knife like a skilled calligrapher, Zhi had the character for 'cloud' quickly carved into the palm. With a dismissive wave from Zhi, Ming was dragged back to his place and dumped and Wen was brought forward.

Zhi played with the knife as he thought. As with Ming, a cloth was forced into Wen's mouth and the palm of his left hand was held forth, one of the thieves grasping his arm to keep him from moving. Zhi carved the character for 'servant' in the palm and then added the character for 'rain' in the other palm. Wen closed his eyes at the brilliant light that coursed through his head. Everything happened with a slowness that seemed otherworldly. One of the women stanched the blood in his palms with the cloth from his mouth. Zhi turned his head to talk to one of his men. He licked the blade of the knife. There was a spot of blood on his upper lip. His tongue darted out, swirled around the drop and disappeared. It seemed as if Zhi were swallowing his own tongue as it slipped back into his mouth. The knife held loosely in his hand, Zhi wiped it on his shirt and inserted it back into his belt.

Two bandits dragged Wen away and dumped him next to Ming, where he lay a long time staring at the sky, his hands clenched against the pain.

The bandits kept drinking, taking great gulps of rice wine from the skins. After a while, one of the men stumbled up from the fire, vomited noisily onto the ground and passed out in the opening of a hut. Another skin was passed to Zhi. He set it aside. "We will take the prisoners now." The sun had set but a sickly pale yellow light still stained the western sky. A full moon rimmed the horizon like a cartwheel rolling across a plain. With no moisture in the air to weigh it down and no wind to move it, the smoke from their fire rose straight into the heavens.

As three of the men lit torches from the fire, Zhi instructed several of the women to bring along the remaining goatskins of wine. The entire party headed into the sepia dusk following a narrow path that threaded deeper into the hills. After a while, Zhi halted and sniffed the air. A slight breeze had come up with the growing night and the full moon had crested the hills, seeming to stare down at them.

As they walked, the youngest of the bandits slid up next to Zhi.

"What are we doing with the prisoners?" Zhi didn't seem to care that Wen and Ming, who walked directly behind him, could hear.

Zhi explained, at times slurring his words from the effects of the wine. "Long ago, when this land was still green, the ancestors were appeased by sacrifices. But now, our pitiful sacrifices fail because we have abandoned the old ways, the ways demanded by Heaven. For three years, we have had little rain. Nothing grows but dust. Our ancestors will not intercede with the gods because our will is weak. A thousand times I have called on our gods to bring rain and nothing has happened. We must return to the old ways of sacrifice. A goat here, a pile of rice there, a few silver coins – they are not enough. We must offer living human flesh. We must offer fearless soldiers to our ancestors, and servants they can use in the other life. We will leave the prisoners in the tomb after we perform the rite the ancestors called the Sealing Up of Green Prayers. You must watch and learn. Tomorrow, when the light returns, we will close up the entrance to the tomb with great stones and bury them alive. It is right. It is what our gods want. It is what our ancestors demand. Once this is done, the rains will return."

"Have you been inside the tomb?" the boy asked.

"It is forbidden to enter the burial mound. I learned from my father who learned from his, and many fathers before them – terrible things will befall us if we desecrate the burial mound."

Wen looked at Zhi walking ahead of him, leading the little band. The man was tall, with grim features that Wen could sense even in the dark, his jaw set, his teeth gritted. His gait was determined. Wen had seen the strange light in his hard joyless eyes. It was the light of fervour. His eyes burned with belief – brilliant, piercing, unbending.

Some time later, when the darkness surrounded them, the stars slicing down from the black heavens, they stopped. The moon, higher and smaller now, silvered the surrounding hills.

They approached a nearby hillock and Wen noticed what appeared to be a piece of stone carving sticking out of the sandy soil at an angle. Passing close to it, he realized it was the head of a horse. *It must have once guarded the approach to the tomb,* he surmised, recalling burial mounds he had visited in the south, where the approaches were lined with stone sculptures of horses, lions, gods and sages.

Before them appeared a ragged opening in the side of the hill, large enough for a man to bow through. Wen realized that it was indeed an ancient tomb, like those he had seen, looted long ago, in his own town. One of the torchbearers leaned into the opening and Zhi yanked him back. "Stay out."

The breeze swirled through the narrow valley between the hills and over the mound with more insistence and Wen felt cool musty air emanating from the tomb.

Zhi's eyes shone in the torchlight as he kowtowed before the opening, touching his forehead to the ground. When he stood again, he called the oldest woman forward, telling her to pour water from a skin into a shallow bowl. In this he washed his hands, drying them on a piece of cloth provided by another woman. He announced: "We will seal the tomb with green prayers."

Zhi began to mumble the prayers and Wen wondered what he might have been before the drought. *A monk? A Taoist priest? A government official?*

At the end, Zhi said: "We deliver these messengers as our sacrifice."

He ordered the prisoners into the tomb, shoving Wen and Ming through the entrance. "Go. Go until you find the ancestors, and do not come out, or we will disembowel you and flay you alive. The entrance will be guarded, so do not even attempt to escape. Do you hear?" Ming could only groan, a stricken look on his face, his body shaking, but Wen, head bowed, said grimly, "We understand." Zhi instructed one of his men to hand Wen a torch and the two prisoners headed down the tunnel, feeling their way into the tomb.

As the light from Wen and Ming's torch disappeared into the depths of the mound, Zhi told his men to start a fire a short distance from the entrance. The brigands and their women gathered and sat in a circle around the fire. More skins of wine were opened and all began to drink again, except for one young woman, their longtime prisoner. Each time the skin was passed to her, she raised it to her lips but drank nothing.

Zhi announced, "Tonight we will celebrate the rains to come, and in the morning light we will move large stones to close up the tomb entrance. But for tonight, drink. This wine was sent by Heaven to let us know that the drought will soon end."

For hours, they kept the wine-filled skins circling, men and women trying to outdo each other, wine flooding into their mouths and out the creased corners of their lips, soaking their clothes and filthy hair. And still the young woman only pretended to drink, seemingly filling her mouth but not allowing a drop to pass down her throat. When, one by one, the bandits passed out on the ground where they sat, she too pretended to fall asleep. With one eye she watched the last two drinkers, Zhi and Hong, finish another skin. Finally, Hong stood, took six steps away from the fire and fell flat on his face, still as a corpse.

"Hong," Zhi shouted, "you scoundrel; you leave me to drink alone?" Standing shakily, he stumbled over to Hong's form and kicked the unmoving body. "Wake up! Drink with me!" But Hong did not move. Zhi slumped down in a heap where he was. He pulled the knife out and waved it around in the air. "Devils!" he shouted once, then fell back heavily onto the ground, and passed out.

The girl lay still, listening and waiting. It was now the middle of the night. The fire had died down to embers. No one had moved for a long while. She opened her eyes and raised her head, looking about. A sleeper grunted and the girl ducked back down, but nothing more happened and she lifted her head again. She got to her knees. None of the bandits shifted, although a young child whimpered and dug for its mother's teat. The young woman watched, and held her breath. Struggling to her feet, she waited. Nothing happened. No one moved. They looked as if they had been slaughtered in their sleep. She took a step, and another, and still no one moved. Grabbing a blackened torch, she stabbed it into the fire, relighting it in the dying embers, and turning away, hurried into the cave.

A short ways down from the entrance, her torch picked up the flickering of jewelled eyes. Soon she came upon the statue of a leaping demon painted blood red, his hair on fire, fangs exposed at the corners of his mouth. She edged around the guardian sculpture and continued down into the burial mound.

"Listen." Wen raised his head. He and Ming sat in the middle of the wide circular room that was the main hall of the tomb, breathing the cold, thick air. Above them, the constellations of the night sky had been painted on the ceiling. All around the edges of the main chamber, eight small anterooms displayed treasures of all sorts. Wen and Ming had hardly noticed the riches around them while searching desperately for another exit, and finding nothing. Statues of jade and gold – soldiers, servants, horses – had reflected their torchlight, vases of coins, sculptures of silver and precious stones, a basket filled with what looked like rice made of gold – none of it meant anything when all they wanted to find was a patch of blackness that led to an exit. Finally, they had collapsed in despair next to a cart that was filled with gold coins, meant to accompany the dead on their journey through the afterlife. There was more gold than Wen and Ming had seen in their lives. Half consciously, Ming had slipped a single gold coin, with the image of a woman's head on one side and a dragon on the other, into his pocket.

Hearts sinking, they sat on the ground next to each other, their torch now flickering with a feeble light. They tried to decide what to do. "I would rather be slaughtered in clean night air than die entombed." Ming had urged, "Let us rush out and take our chances with the swords of the bandits."

But Wen had hesitated. "Wait. Let me think," he had said, and so they sat.

A moment later, Wen said, "Listen."

Ming raised his head. "Someone is coming." He said it in a neutral way, staring towards the entrance to the tunnel.

The flickering light of a torch could be seen – then a hand reaching out as if trying to part the darkness. Wen and Ming stood and looked in amazement at the wide-eyed girl from Jinhan, her face flushed and reflecting the flames of the torch.

"How…?" Wen shook his head.

"I was their prisoner. They are all dead drunk. I only pretended to drink with them and pretended to pass out. One by one, they toppled over, even the young mothers. When I rose and took a torch, no one moved." She turned to Ming. "I recognized you from Jinhan."

Ming nodded. "I have seen you there as well."

The girl hung her head. "My name is Ying. They captured me many months ago. I long to see my parents, my sisters. Several times, when food was low, they almost decided to kill me, but Zhi would not allow it. His woman has not provided him a son. He longs for a son."

Wen said: "Will it be safe to leave?"

"Yes, but we must go quickly, though I believe none of them will wake now for a while. It is the first time they have found wine in the time I have been with them and they have lost the ability to hold it. It tramples them into the ground. Even Zhi."

Wen said, "We will extinguish the torch and leave in darkness."

"Then to the camp, where the horses are tied." Ying was already hurrying up the tunnel.

At the mouth of the tomb, they hesitated. No one around the dying fire shifted. With a tight grip on Wen's forearm to hold him back, Ming whispered urgently, "The gold. We could take some. They are all asleep. Let us go back for the gold!"

The girl was already edging out of the cave in the dark. Wen hissed, "Forget the gold. We must leave! Come!"

The three shadows skirted the drunken forms lying about on the ground – Wen snatched up his knife as he passed Zhi – and hurried down the trail for the camp.

At the camp, they gathered up several bags of rice and skins of water and loaded them onto three horses, untying and scattering the other horses into the darkness.

As they were about to leave, Wen found his dao sword on the ground. Meanwhile, Ming searched quickly for his sword but could not find it.

"Hurry!" Wen called.

In moments, they were flying back along the trail toward Jinhan, following the girl. When they came to the narrow defile where Wen had shrugged off his pack, he searched desperately, riding among the low bushes, holding them back with his sword as he leaned down from his horse. Thanks to the brightness of the moonlight, he found it. Wen tied his pack onto the horse, while he and Ming said farewell to the girl.

"I hope the rest of your journey is easily accomplished," Ying said, sitting high and straight on her horse, "and that one day you will both have the good fortune to return to the land of your ancestors." She looked at Ming when she said this.

"You saved our lives," Wen said. "We owe you much. Once you reach the town, you will be safe within its walls. May the gods protect you."

She turned, dug her heels into the horse and rode hard for Jinhan.

Wen mounted and prepared to ride on. "Come, we must hurry," he said to Ming, who was still staring after the girl.

They turned about and rode through the remainder of the night, north and east across the dry lands under the bleak unquestioning moon.

∼

Wen and Ming fled the rolling brown hills and barren countryside, riding hard for two days in a northeasterly direction. Eventually, the fields began to grow faintly green with spindly grass and greener still as they approached a broad river in the distance. Drawing closer to the riverbank, they noticed that water filled only the central channel of the river's usual course, though it was of such a depth and width that it still required the use of a small ferry to cross. A short trot downriver brought the pair to the ferryboat landing where several dozen peasants waited and where a small, impromptu market had assembled. Before boarding the ferry, Wen was able to arrange for the sale of the two horses.

"Why sell the horses?" Ming questioned.

"I was instructed by my teacher to walk to the Emperor's capital, not ride. In any case, we would arrive too soon at Linan if we traveled by horse for the remainder of our journey. I must not reach Linan before late summer. I have two more paintings to accomplish in the meantime. But, most importantly, riding would change my relationship to the landscape. I must immerse myself completely in the natural world if I am going to paint it, if I am going to apprehend and express its spirit. I must feel within me the iciness of every stream, the upward surge of the pines, the hardness of stone and the softness of mist. One cannot do this by riding by, hurrying to one's destination."

"It was an excellent horse," Ming sighed when the spirited beast was led away, tossing its head to and fro.

After the quick crossing – the ferry consisting of little more than a wooden raft controlled by groups of men on each shore pulling on ropes – Wen and Ming bought food and drink at an inn on the far side of the river. They feasted on flat bread – silver and glittering and fresh from the water – rice cooked in large leathery leaves, and drank rice wine flavoured with pepper.

After eating, they inquired concerning the direction to the capital. The innkeeper stepped out the door and pointed up past the small roof-pines growing from the soil accumulated between the tiles of his tavern roof. "Through that range of peaks and into the green rice country beyond. Unlike us, they have had plenty of rain. Their children are fat. You should eat well there. Last autumn's harvest was good." The innkeeper sounded as if he wanted to join them. "But it is far to the capital city. Distant as the moon. It will take you months to reach it on foot."

"That is good," said Wen. "We are in no hurry."

The range of peaks was narrow and scored by deep valleys so Wen and Ming were not required to climb over high mountain passes to reach the far side. They spent the next several days ascending a trail that climbed from the valley floor, crossing shallow streams that came coursing down from the heights. From the high mountainside, they could see the foothills and broad valley beyond, infused with the moist green light of spring. Finally, they were leaving the brown, burnt lands behind. Hiking through a valley, they saw on the hillside above, in the crowns of poplars and maples, a dusting of leaves like green stars brushed against a blue sky. Sunlight poured down on them, barely shadowed by the limbs of the high trees and their unfolding buds.

Each evening, while Ming built a fire and cooked, Wen pulled out paper and charcoal and sketched scenes he had glimpsed that day during their walk: a smooth rock the size of a water buffalo, a jagged peak, dishevelled ghosts of morning mist drifting through crowns of spruce, a forest of ancient bamboo, a stand of young cypresses.

After three days, the path began to descend and after half a day's hike more, they came to a high clearing that overlooked the valley. Far below, flooded rice paddies reflected the strong spring sun. In the distance stood a village, smoke curling like pigs' tails from huts.

From where they stood, Wen and Ming could discern far to their left and high above them, the line of peaks disappearing west, the faces of the mountains and their foothills covered with pine and spruce forests that appeared soft and dark as wet fur. These were interspersed with patches of deciduous trees in feathery green bloom. On gentle lower slopes, terraces of rice paddies echoed the contour of the hills, like the ripple of water before the wind. Directly below them, a narrow river hugged the foothills and, after a wide curve, fanned out into several channels in the flat valley beyond.

Paddies lined the river in the distance where hundreds of farmers in conical hats were bent over, transplanting rice seedlings. Other farmers dumped baskets of grey cooking ash into the paddies as fertilizer. In a few places along the riverbank, where the ground rose higher, lines of plum trees had unfolded into bloom and willows dragged their yellow-green fronds in the water's blue-green stream. Further off, fields in shades of jade and emerald shone in patches that resembled garments of silk. A family of crows flew squawking through a stand of tall spindly spruce directly below them.

Wen gazed out toward the paddies again. "The beauty of spring – it mocks the farmers in their season of hunger."

"But the innkeeper said the babies here are fat. There must be plenty of food."

"I am sure he was referring to last autumn. Spring always remains a time of hunger for farmers, when supplies of rice run low."

"Yes, it was true in Jinhan as well. Even in good years, spring was hard."

"Spring, especially after the Startling-of-the-Insects time, is always difficult. Plum blossoms feed only poets."

They noted, far below, the shadow of a cloud rippling across the earth and a breeze shirring the water of the paddies. Nearby where they stood, a waterfall rushed down the rocks, its white foam resembling a stream of tumbling orchids.

"Look." Ming pointed into the thick forest. Wen followed his finger and he too saw the well-worn trail there, disappearing into deep shadow. The warm breeze of spring sighed through the trees and occasionally brought to them the faint sound of an iron bell.

"Do you hear it?"

Ming nodded. "Perhaps it is a monastery."

"Perhaps." Wen had his eyes closed, listening.

The gonging of the rustic bell drifted amidst birdsong and the pulsations of the wind. Wen opened his eyes and watched a stronger breeze below rip through a stand of plum trees, releasing a powdery cloud of pollen. In the swishing of the stronger wind, the muted sound of the bell was lost.

Wen, removing his pack and setting it on the ground, turned to Ming. "This is a harmonious place. We will stay here for a few days while I paint."

"What shall I do while you work?"

"You are free to watch and learn, if you have the interest; or, if not, you can do as you wish – explore the hills and nearby villages." Wen paused. "On second thought, Ming, why don't you go down into the fields and help the farmers?"

"Yes. I could help." He turned to regard the distant paddies. "I am not a painter, nor a poet. My back is strong. I will help the farmers plant rice."

"Yes. That is good." Wen watched the workers far below labouring through the paddies up to their mid-calves in water and mud. "You know, Ming, there are many more poems in the ancient annals about drinking rice wine than planting rice. Perhaps there should be more poems about planting rice."

That evening, they made a fire and cooked their meal, and again heard the faint tolling of the iron bell, as if it were beckoning them. They looked but saw no one down the forested slopes or on the well-worn path.

"Listen." Wen cocked his head, and put his hand behind his ear. The iron bell rang again, reverberating and echoing through gorges and shadowy forest. "When a monastery bell rings in the mountains, it rings from everywhere: from the crowns of the pines and their trunks, from the stones, from the stream at our feet and from distant peaks, from every leaf and needle, from sun and moon, from mist and ink-wash clouds, from stars and the black spaces between them. Once rung, it goes on ringing. Who knows when it ends?"

By dusk, the valley had filled with mist, and the mountains and foothills around them were festooned with ribbons of fog that twined through the majestic pines and spruce and hid the uppermost range of peaks.

Wen prepared to sleep. *Tomorrow is the Festival of Cold Food. In the morning, I will make offerings of rice, tea leaves and incense to my ancestors.* He gazed about him to try to allay his sadness at being far from home. Throughout the journey, he had managed to avoid succumbing to the sorrow of his memories – of his dead father and a few relatives in the town, of One Tooth and the monastery – out of fear that these thoughts would become a burden to him, perhaps even forcing him to abandon his duty. But, today, on this festival day, it was impossible.

Not far off, a great pine tree, forty spans around, thrust itself into the heavens. At the end of a branch, a quarter-moon floated on its back, with three stars in a triangle directly above. It looked like a small boat, and this too reminded him of home. From the chill twilight suddenly came the earthy scent of ink to change his mood. *It is a good sign; a sign that tomorrow I will paint.*

As Wen fell into sleep, he delighted in the fresh air warm and damp with spring. *This is a site of great harmony*, he thought, drifting, *but heaven can turn to hell in a moment.* He knew it could come as quickly and simply as a tumble off a cliff or a tiger entering their camp. *And what about the message? Who would deliver the message to the Emperor then?*

But heaven didn't turn to hell. It proved to be an excellent location, with a view that inspired his hunger to paint. The next morning, with no fire and eating only cold food as prescribed by the ritual for the festival, Ming joined Wen in making offerings to their ancestors. Afterward, bursting with good spirits and vigour, Ming headed down the slope.

"Return in seven days," Wen said. "I will be finished by then, and I will have a new painting to show you."

Ming turned and hurried down toward the morning fields where thin ghosts of mist arose from the river and dissolved in sunlight.

~

Standing, looking at the valley below, Wen held in his hand the small bamboo brush that contained the message for the Emperor. For a moment he thought he might fling it off the cliff, be rid of the burden of it and wander freely ever after, but the feeling passed.

Beneath him, the wind was raking through the pines, tumbling through their crowns. He considered the wind's invisible presence as it weaved through leaves and branches, making pine needles and the distant reeds flicker with light, its activity recognized only by its effect. *Nothing pleases my heart more than the action of the wind,* he thought. *It seems to be a metaphor for something essential in life, but I am not sure what. Perhaps it's a symbol for the spirit of the world, and for the individual breath.*

Something there is that moves through the world, inexpressible, apprehended but unseen, sensed but beyond sense. A message without shape or form, never spoken and therefore never heard, known only by its effects, and yet a message of utter clarity, the world arising in itself, coming to birth in the light of its own light, a wind in a shining mirror, the sky in a lake. The luminous moment inseparable from the brilliance of eternity – a message to itself.

Staring at the brush held between thumb and index finger, Wen realized that his reason for delivering the message had changed. At first, he had wanted to please his teacher, to fulfill the wishes of One Tooth. With that view, over time the duty had become a burden. Now he discovered – like the silkworm that creates its own cocoon, its world – that he wanted to deliver the message for himself.

Wen sat on the ground and looked out over the valley for half the morning. He wasn't thinking about the painting, he was simply emptying himself, making a space for the world below. A songbird speckled the breeze that flowed through the trees, lifting the pine boughs and letting them down again. To the west, the long chain of mountains shivered in waves.

Spreading out a sheet of paper, he gathered his sketches, brushes and inks. Once he had weighted the paper at the corners with small stones, he again sat and stared at its emptiness, holding his tiny brush of silk strands above the page. *The blank sheet is the greatest work*, he reflected, *because all the paintings of the future are hidden there. The blank page can accommodate anything, move in any of the ten directions with ease, invisibly, as natural as the growth of a tree branch, as natural as the curve of a river shining with light, as the slope of a mountain appearing out of the mist of dawn. The entire world is there – in the mirror of the blank sheet. The blank page is more than the sum of all worlds, and yet – it is nothing.*

Setting aside the silk strand brush, he added water to the turtle shell, and ground the ink, thinking of nothing but the feel of the shell and the ink stick slipping. Finally, he dipped and swirled his brush in the minute and glittering black pool cupped in his hand and began to work.

He read the landscape with a painter's eye. He knew his ink and paper intimately, knew exactly how much water to add to make the rice fields glisten, exactly how much liquid the paper would absorb, how much ink was required to paint the stand of dark pines, how to turn the brush to replicate a branch, a leaf, a stone, a peak. The ink stick itself was made of burnt pine – the dead pines in the ink would come back to life in the painting of pines. He knew that black ink was a blend of all colours, contained them all. The world was already painted.

The vast landscape began to appear as a simple range of tonal variations: the pattern of patchwork fields and paddies was echoed in the striations of bark in pines and oaks, in the patterns of shadow and light on the higher slopes, in patches of lichen and moss on rocks, the mottling of a leaf, of a springtime rabbit's fur, of a partridge's wings.

For Wen, every element of nature was a brush stroke. His mind, his eye, the world, his hand, the brush, the voice and instructions of his teacher, all his previous paintings and the paintings he admired, joined in perfect harmony.

Ink flowed up the boles of the trees, out every branch to the tips of their light-gathering needles, ink made mountains appear.

Ink turned into rivers and clouds as the wind swirled his effortless brush. Ink made the world visible. It was the world's blood rushing to the surface of its skin.

～

When Ming returned from the valley after seven days, Wen showed him the painting, which was hanging from a tree branch, drying.

Ming gestured at the characters that descended in a line from near the top of the painting. "What does the poem say?"

Wen read it aloud.

Far below in the valley
Farmers plant rice seedlings
In the glistening water
Between their feet

After labouring all day
Under the powerful sun
They will get drunk on rice wine
And sing ancient songs about planting rice

"It is true." said Ming, "First, leaning forward all day to plant, then leaning back half the night to drink." He paused and thought a moment. "They told me that a crazy abbot heads the monastery. When we begin our descent tomorrow, will we stop there?"

Wen nodded.

Again Ming gazed at the painting and the calligraphy of the poem. "Here, the dot looks like a dropped rock, and here like a fallen orchid, and here, the horizontal stroke resembles a shred of spring cloud." After a few moments, he pointed at a mountain: "It is impossible. You reveal the shady side of the mountain and its sunlit face at the same time."

"Yes."

"Why?"

"Because the painting is not limited by time, nor is it limited to a single view but includes all views at once. For the creative to be born, for the intangible to be made visible, masculine and feminine, the light and the dark, absence and presence, must be brought together."

"And there is mist in the gorges but sunlight in the valley for the same reason?"

"Yes."

"There," Ming pointed again. "That figure who walks along the river as it curls in and out among the trees. He has a pack on his back. Is it you?"

"It is."

"And next to him, the other figure?"

"It's you, Ming."

"So, you have traced our journey from the dry lands all the way to here, and beyond. It is like a map."

"Exactly."

Ming gazed at the painted landscape in silence, then closed his eyes. "I hear it in the painting."

"How so?"

"The sound of the bell."

Late that night, long after Wen had fallen asleep, Ming arose and extracted the painting of spring from the bamboo tube where Wen had stored it once it had dried. He sat staring at it, noting how it subtly depicted their journey since they had left Jinhan, came through the dry lands and were entombed by the bandits. In the bottom left corner of the painting, he traced their trail by following the features depicted there: the mound of the tomb almost invisible, the river they crossed, a towering waterfall at the foot of the mountains. Then he followed their journey across the painting as it revealed the valley of rice paddies below.

For the remainder of their journey, every few weeks Ming

would secretly remove the painting of spring and study it, ensuring he could remember the way back.

∾

Li Wen's eyes opened wide on a brilliant morning. Above him, young leaves the colour of green water shivered and sparked with light in a high breeze against a spacious blue sky. Wen heard Ming shunting about collecting bits of wood, and glimpsed him appearing and disappearing from the corner of his view. When he saw the first flames leaping, Wen arose to the sound of crackling branches.

Wen approached his friend who was squatting near the fire, concentrating on something in his hand. He was turning it over and over, captivated by its gleam,

"You took a gold coin from the cave?"

Ming looked up at Wen standing over him and squinted from the sunlight. "One. I took only one."

"You regret not taking more?"

Ming shrugged and turned back to the fire, speaking into the flames. "We will walk down to the monastery today?"

"I suspect we will pass it on the trail to the valley, in any case."

"As I said, the farmers in the paddies told me the abbot of the monastery is a crazy monk."

"Soon we will meet him and decide for ourselves."

As they hiked along the trail later that day, crossing several rickety bridges and tree trunks thrown over streams and passing through a stand of towering cinnamon trees, they came upon several sheer rock faces that had poems chiselled into them. One, near a waterfall, displayed huge characters that read, "a waterfall's thousand foot stream / unfolds like a cascade of silk".

As they descended, they glimpsed the monastery through a stand of bamboo. In order to approach it, they had to cross another stream and here they saw a monk standing up to his knees in water, leaning on a bamboo staff and holding up his robes to keep them from getting wet. Instead of the usual shaved head, the monk had long glistening black hair that hung down each side of his face almost to his waist. He stood staring down at the water, transfixed, gazing at the stream that curled around his legs and disappeared behind him.

"Greetings, friend," Wen called, but the monk was undisturbed and did not look up. He appeared to be staring at his own reflection in the water. Wen and Ming glanced at each other. "Perhaps he is deaf," Wen said. "Friend monk, will you take us to your abbot?"

The clean-shaven monk continued staring into the passing water, then mumbled to himself.

"What's that you say?" asked Wen.

"The knife that can cut itself is the one to be revered." The monk kept his head down.

The two travellers started to leave, thinking they would go into the monastery and inquire there. They turned away, and the monk, still contemplating the water at his feet, announced: "You cannot truly enter the mountains unless you first enter the stream."

Again, Wen and Ming eyed each other and shrugged their shoulders. Kicking off their straw sandals, they stepped into the icy water of the stream. Wen asked, "Will you now take us to your abbot?"

The monk looked up and smiled. The trio climbed from the stream onto the path and the monk paused. "Do you hear the birds?" A rich brocade of birdsong filtered through the forest, sounding like wood knocking and water bubbling.

Led by the monk, they entered the courtyard of the monastery. Beside the dharma hall, two bald-headed young monks were tending a fire under an iron tripod kettle. They bowed to the long-haired monk who approached them and announced, "We have two guests," adding, "Bring wine and food."

"Yes, Master."

Wen realized that the long-haired monk they were following must himself be the abbot. He led them through an open doorway into a spacious hall with thick woven bamboo mats on the floor and bade them have a seat. The pavilion had a roof but was open on the sides.

Ming and Wen removed their packs and sat.

"Welcome to the Temple of Accumulated Incense. I am Abbot Kuan."

"Of what sect are you?" Wen asked.

"I live in the Sixth House of Ch'an."

A quizzical look crossed Wen's face. "The Sixth House? It is my understanding that there are but Five Houses of Ch'an offering five ways to attain perfection. I have never heard of this Sixth House."

The abbot grinned, showing overlarge teeth and high cheekbones. "The Sixth House is whatever is outside all the others. It has the same relationship to the Five Houses of Ch'an as the sky and the earth have to ordinary houses."

Wen nodded, while Ming scratched his head and looked around at the room, which was constructed of pine boards that gave off a pleasant odour of fresh cut wood. To the east, he noted a path of white stones disappearing into the forest. To the west, a red rock, the size of a man, had been installed near the pavilion. The rock looked vaguely like a sitting Buddha.

"Ah, the wine." The abbot glanced up as the two young monks bowed at the doorway and entered carrying trays with pots of steaming rice wine and a basket of nuts. They also bore three bowls of congee with bits of salted duck egg and bamboo shoots and a sprinkling of green onion. They placed the bowls and pots of wine on a low thick wooden table before the trio.

Through the long afternoon, they drank wine, ate and talked. The abbot was anxious to hear of their travels, where they had been and what they had seen. At the mention of Wen's master, One Tooth, the abbot said, "Ah, yes, I know him. By reputation only. We have never met. And you say he's given you a message to take to the Emperor? What are the contents of this message?"

"I remain ignorant of its contents since I am forbidden to

look at it. One Tooth's command was that the message was for the Emperor's eyes alone."

The abbot was silent while they ate. Finally, he said, "You say you are an artist? Did your master ever ask you to draw his portrait?"

Wen was surprised at the question. "Yes, a week before I began this journey, he requested just that. He appeared quite pleased with the result."

Wen knew that for a master to ask an artist to paint his portrait was a sign of respect. Abbot Kuan nodded and it seemed to Wen, from that point on, he treated him differently. Kuan said, "I too am a painter."

As they continued the story of their travels, by unspoken agreement neither Ming nor Wen mentioned the tomb but included other details about their run-in with the bandits in the dry lands. The abbot said, "I have known bandits like that. In fact, once, long ago, I myself was one. We would slit a man's throat for a palmful of rice, for looking at us the wrong way. I have spent years atoning for my youthful wrongdoing. You are extremely fortunate to be alive."

Ming's sleepy eyes sparkled with an idea. "Master, tell us what you know of immortality."

"Immortality? Pah! A delusion! A complete and utter fabrication!" The anger of the drink surfaced in the abbot for a moment – but then he laughed.

"What are you?" the abbot asked Ming. "A Taoist? A Buddhist? What?"

"A peasant farmer," he said.

The three talked and drank until dusk began to stain the sky. The abbot showed the effects of the wine less at first than the others, despite his having downed twice as many cups. To Wen, it seemed his eyes grew brighter and clearer the more he drank.

He began singing an ancient tune:

Once my tongue and throat are moist with wine
And my belly full as a t'ing vessel,

Ink flows from my eyes and fingers,
Spurts from the hole in my heart —
Rocks and pines, rivers and mountains without end
Appear on white walls, across the heavens,
Arise like dreams.

He stopped and stared at Wen, who considered it odd that the abbot had concluded the poem at seven lines instead of the standard eight. He wondered if this was a sure sign of madness in a poet. The abbot's gaze was serious and Wen felt uncomfortable under his stare. The actions of the abbot seemed unpredictable. Perhaps there was some truth to the rice farmers' warning that he was crazy. The abbot asked, "What do you think might be in that message for the Emperor?"

Wen hesitated. He didn't really want to discuss the message. "I know not."

"Are you not tempted to read it?"

"Yes, of course. At times the urge comes upon me just before sleep, or while walking hour after hour on the trail. I cannot help but wonder: what exactly is it that One Tooth wants to tell the Emperor, what is it that I am spending so much time and effort delivering? But my duty is to deliver it only."

"Of course, you are bringing the paintings too. You say you have completed three?"

"Yes."

"Show them to me."

Wen, glad to avoid further discussion about the message for the Emperor, bowed and said, "I would be honoured." He proceeded to pull the large bamboo tube from his pack and extract the three paintings, spreading them out on the floor. The abbot instructed his attendants to bring stones to weigh down the corners.

Abbot Kuan spent a long time studying the works, pacing back and forth before them. He stopped, stared down at the painting of autumn, closed his eyes in contemplation, opened them again, as if taking the painting in whole. Then he gazed at the landscape beyond the monastery walls and turned again to look at the painting. He did the same with the paintings of winter and spring. Finally he turned to Wen. "I cannot say if you are an accomplished Buddhist," Kuan concluded, "but you are certainly a painter." He gazed again at the most recent painting, the one of spring just completed on the mountain slope above them. Wen and Ming studied it along with him.

"What is the name of this region where we are now?" Wen asked.

"It is called Jui-chou."

"And the mountain we are on?"

"Mount Tung."

Recalling their earlier trek over the mountain, Ming spoke, his eyes heavy and dark with the drink. "The peaks of this region are exceptional. It is a beautiful mountain, this Mount Tung."

"It is not the peaks of mountains that are important," the abbot said. "After all, we cannot reach the peaks but can merely admire them from afar. The path through the mountains is what matters."

"Do you think mountains are sacred?" asked Ming.

The abbot nodded. "Yes. All sentient and non-sentient beings are sacred."

"That leaves little else," Ming observed.

"That leaves *nothing* else," Kuan countered.

"All *non-sentient* beings as well?" Wen examined the abbot's face. "Perhaps they are sacred but they cannot expound the teachings."

"O, but they can – and do. By simply 'displaying the ultimate' they expound the teachings."

"How so?"

"It is simple. Trees expound the teachings by sprouting new leaves and losing them again. The sun, by emptying itself into light. Rain, by falling, and the sands of the desert by scattering before the wind. Stones, by glistening when wet and by remaining still, as if listening. The birds expound the teachings by singing at the right time. A pile of shit expounds the teachings by revealing the tracks of flies, by its shape and smell. The earth expounds the teachings by accepting whatever falls onto it; the cup…" he lifted his drinking cup, "by keeping its mouth wide open and ready; the knife by staying sharp or going dull with use, and reflecting light; and the mirror expounds the teachings by accepting whatever arises." He drank. "That is how non-sentient beings 'display the ultimate' and expound the teachings."

"My journeys have taught me one thing," Wen concluded. "All spiritual paths merge in nature because nature is their ultimate source. The original voices of all the teachers can be heard in the gurgling brook, in the high wind among the leaves, in that birdsong we heard earlier by the stream."

"This is true." Picking up a wooden stick, the abbot clacked it sharply once on the wooden table before him, making Ming jump. One of the young monks came to the doorway, bowed and turned away. A moment later he was back with a stoneware pitcher brimming with black ink and a thick roll of paper the colour of rice powder, while a second attendant carried a lacquered tray piled with brushes of various sizes.

The monk unrolled the paper on the floor from one end of the pavilion to the other.

"Come," Kuan ordered as he stood and stumbled over to the pitcher. Grasping and lifting the pitcher, he poured a thick stream of ink into a wide shallow porcelain bowl. Taking his long hair in his left hand and twirling it, he tied a ribbon near the bottom, leaving a length of hair at the end gathered like a brush. This he dipped into the bowl and swirled about soaking up the black pigment. In a bizarre dance, holding his hair in his hand like a brush and swaying his head back and forth, he began covering the paper with calligraphic strokes. Wen and Ming watched him work his way, trance-like, across the room, dipping his hair again and again and brushing strokes onto the sheet. When he came to the end, one of the young attendants arrived with a bowl filled with water in which the abbot dunked his hair. He then wiped his hair many times with a cloth.

When finished, Kuan poured himself a full cup of wine and slung it straight down his throat. He seemed to have forgotten the presence of his visitors. Another cupful shot down his gullet. He threw the porcelain cup across the room and burst into song, another ancient ballad, but the words were so slurred that Wen couldn't distinguish one from the next. The abbot went to the collection of brushes on the tray, chose the largest one—about the size of a baby's arm—plunged it into the ink and slopped it onto the paper sheet, over his previous work. Dropping to his knees, he let go of the brush and slid both hands through the puddle of ink, singing in a loud voice. Then he shouted, wiped his hands on a clean spot on the paper and clapped them together.

Ming stared in astonishment, while Wen leaned closer and observed.

Outside a storm was gathering, thunder rupturing the sky, the roar of boulders rolling down a mountain and bursting open. Kuan noticed, paused a moment, turning his head at the sound. Picking up a brush again, he swished it about, adding more ink, working without care, spattering ink everywhere, using his bare feet to spread the ink in patches, his hands to swirl it, the various brushes now to work it across the entire expanse of paper, never once ceasing to sing or shout or laugh or babble incoherently, stumbling and spinning about as he attacked the canvas with an energy Wen had never before witnessed in a painter. Ming stood with his gaze fixed on the abbot, stunned, fearful of the manic display before him.

Finally, Kuan grunted and tumbled over, collapsing onto the floor, face down on a bamboo mat – and passed out.

Thunder rumbled above and a crack of lightning was followed by a hard driving rain that fell straight down, dripping from the roof in lines like a beaded curtain. Wen and Ming edged up to the painting. The flurry of activity and the flailing of the abbot had kept them from seeing the details of what he had created.

Wen was shocked at the clarity of the horizontal landscape before him. It vibrated with energy. He marvelled at the fresh, exuberant line of the stream that flowed at the foot of a chain of mountains stretching across the scroll, disappearing and reappearing among the trees. At the end, a vertical series of written characters concluded the painting with a poem.

Wen leaned over the calligraphy and read aloud for Ming's benefit what the abbot had written.

Before entering the mountains
you must enter the stream that reflects the mountains

This old monk's face too
shines in a pool of ink

The knife that can cut itself
is the one to be revered

Wen and Ming spent the night at the monastery. The next morning, preparing to leave Mount Tung, they came upon Abbot Kuan, looking fresh and bright, standing by the fire in the courtyard, feeding his long painting into the flames.

Ming spoke, a look of confusion on his face. "You are burning your work – why?"

The abbot grunted, offering no answer. Lifting his gaze to the sky, he watched the black smoke dissolve and disappear.

Shouldering their packs and taking their leave, Wen and Ming followed the stream down through the foothills, until they came into the broad valley chequered with rice paddies.

∽

Throughout the day, Wen and Ming followed the narrow tracks among the paddies, crossing the broad valley in the rising heat.

Unable to travel in a direct line, they were forced to follow the layout of the paddies – some long and narrow, others rectangular or squarish – and to walk along the complex of paths which necessitated constant turns this way and that – now east, now west, now north or south – to negotiate around the standing pools where the young rice seedlings had been planted.

Wen was burdened by a thoughtful, melancholic mood, adding to the weight of his pack. Skirting the paddies, he could glimpse his somber reflection in the shallow waters as he walked. He hoped Ming did not take his silence to mean he had done something to offend. Ming would greet peasants they passed, a few of whom recognized him from the time he had spent planting rice. Ming did not appear bothered by Wen's silence but seemed to accept it without question.

After experiencing the exquisite painting and calligraphy of the abbot, Wen was questioning his own artistic worth. *The abbot exhibited such energy, such brilliance – by comparison it makes me feel that my own work amounts to no more than the dull scratching of a chicken in a farmyard.*

In mid-afternoon, Wen broke his silence. "Ming, tell me, what did you think of the artistry of the abbot?"

Ming thought a moment. "The work of the abbot monk was like nothing I have ever seen – not that I have seen much of painting in my life. But I truly believe yours is its equal. The styles are opposed but, for me, both are good."

Wen listened, then a rueful smile came to his face. "Thank you, Ming. You have reminded me of something, an important lesson I had forgotten. Some years ago, my master asked me to paint the south wall of the great hall at the monastery, while a famous painter from the capital who had arrived in our city was asked to decorate the north wall. I was young and energetic and flew at the wall like a man possessed by a gang of demons. In a few short days, I completed the work. I was surprised to find on finishing my wall that the master painter from the capital had barely begun his. I regretted my haste, as the famed artist laboured day after day, constructing and refining a mountain scene that seemed to arise from the wall itself. For a month, I watched him and fretted, constantly comparing my work to his.

"My work, I knew, was light, thoughtless, full of energy and action, and spirited. His was deep, rich with the experience of life, weighty, and meaningful. When it came to judge the two works, One Tooth pointed his staff at my wall and said the pines were simply pines and the mountain peaks were no more than mountain peaks. When he stood before the northern wall done by the other painter, he said, *These pines are much more than pines, and the mountains here are much more than mountains.* He declared that they were both masterful works. He added, however, that he preferred the lightness of the south wall although he could appreciate the great art of the northern wall as well. *I prefer the ordinary,* he said. *Pines really are no more than pines, mountain peaks no more than mountain peaks.*" Wen paused. "The next day, the painter from the capital leapt to his death from a nearby cliff."

"Why would he do that?"

"Because he could not accept that art of differing styles can be great in different ways. And you, Ming, have reminded me of that."

Wen walked the rest of that day giving little further thought to the work of the abbot, and when he did recall it, he appreciated it for what it was in its own right, without making any comparison to his own landscapes.

That night, they slept on the path among the paddies. In the muggy air, mosquitoes by the thousands tortured them, ensuring that neither gained a decent rest. Normally, Wen would have built a smouldering fire and slept in the aura of its smoke to keep the pests away. But there was nothing on the paths to burn and so they suffered, finally crawling under a low tent of blankets to escape. When they awoke at first light, sweating under their makeshift huts, Wen stuck his head out and saw that a thick fog had settled on the valley.

"Perhaps it will clear when the sun grows strong," he said to Ming whose face, like his own, was mottled with bites.

But it didn't clear. They walked for hours, growing confused by the mist. They wandered like lost spirit-beings. The occasional voices they heard came to them disembodied. Wen thought he heard the voice of his father then. He stopped, turned and tried to see back across the paddies. He remembered his father had been calling from his boat, lost in fog on the river. Wen was a young boy standing on the shore. He looked out and could see nothing. "Call to me so I can find the way," his father had shouted. "Here," Wen had shouted back. "I am here." Finally Wen saw the tip of the boat not ten paces away touching the shore. Wen ran to his father and threw his arms around his legs.

As he was recalling this event, Wen nearly collided with an old man coming out of the grey-white wall of fog. His head was tilted slightly back and at first it appeared as if his eyes had themselves been bathed and blanked by the fog.

Wen and Ming made their presence known. The old man wagged his head back and forth. "I do not recognize your voices. You are travellers?"

"Yes," Ming replied, "we are from the south and are going to the capital to see the Emperor."

Wen stared at the man, who was holding a basket made of woven reeds. "Where are you headed?"

"I am searching for my grandsons, who are planting in the paddies, but they were not where I had expected them to be. I have dumplings for them to eat."

Ming asked: "Are you lost because of the fog?"

The old man turned toward the sound of Ming's voice. "I am blind. Fog, no fog – it matters not."

"Of course," Ming said, bowing his head. "Perhaps it is your grandsons who are lost."

"You travellers must be hungry. Let us enjoy some of the dumplings. I am tired of calling and searching and must rest." He slumped down.

Wen and Ming sat too, and the old man handed them each a dumpling. They were soft and doughy on the outside and had a clot of spicy sweet chopped pork at the centre.

They had two fat dumplings each from the basket, eating in silence. Wen wiped the back of his hand across his mouth when finished. "You are most generous. I fear your grandsons will be disappointed when they find we have eaten their meal."

The old man stood, felt about for his basket, lifted it and prepared to leave. "I have never been to the capital, but I am sure it is in that direction." He pointed ahead the way that Wen and Ming had been travelling.

Ming asked, "How can you know the way with certainty?"

"I can smell it—the dumplings there are made using a rare spice. I hear the sighing in the brothels and the rumbling of ten thousand carts on the cobbles."

"But you cannot see it."

The blind man spoke in the direction of Wen. "No, I cannot. And yet I form a picture of the capital and the Emperor in my mind, as do you. None of us knows what we will meet on the way. If you have never seen the Emperor or his city, you are as blind to them as I." He turned away. "I wish you good fortune." Using a walking stick to feel the way ahead, he shuffled off, calling into the fog for his grandsons: "Tao. Shang. Tao. Shang. Tao… Shang…"

Wen and Ming strode ahead, energized from the good rich dumplings. They walked a long while in silence. The fog stayed close to the ground and it seemed they were making good time through the maze of paddies in their attempt to cross the broad valley.

Wen, who was leading the way as they trekked single file on the narrow paths, halted. He gazed about, trying to see through the fog. "This spot looks familiar."

"How so?"

Wen stared straight down at the path. "We slept here last night."

"We have gone in a circle?"

"I fear so."

They slumped down onto the ground and rested. The fog began to thicken and grow dark.

"We will sleep here again. Perhaps by tomorrow the fog will have lifted."

Ming didn't complain. Wen was surprised and pleased that he never expressed a single regret for having come on this difficult and seemingly endless journey. He wondered if Ming still thought about the gold they had left behind in the caves, and if those riches continued to captivate his mind. *With a few of those gold coins, we could have hired a palanquin and been carried across the valley of rice paddies by porters who know the way. Perhaps I have been a fool.*

Just before he fell into sleep, Wen had an image of the letter from his master, Fu Wei, to the Emperor. Wen imagined himself unrolling the small scroll but it tumbled into a paddy where sprouts poked through it and curled into strokes of green calligraphy. Wen fell into a deeper sleep before he could discern any of its characters.

夏
[Summer]

Emperor's Cliff

THE CURATOR OF CHINESE ART stares at Li Wen's painting of summer: a massive cliff ribbed with chasms, a single white stream appearing and disappearing as it threads down the left side, descending the mountain in short courses and small waterfalls. The way it falls feels like music. A piano *diminuendo*.

For a long time he considers the work, alternately focusing on a detail with the binocular loupes or removing the glasses and sitting back to regard it again as a whole, then putting them on again when other details catch his attention. He understands that a Chinese landscape is a 'constructed' world – assembled out of bits and pieces that have captured the artist's interest, combining a unique pine tree here, a rock there, a bush, a hill, a lake in the distance, a granite peak. It is nothing less than an unceasing effort to reveal nature's spirit of harmony, while striving to appear effortless.

A light mist can be seen floating down from the heights, a breath of moisture. He closes his eyes to imagine it caressing his skin. When he opens them again, something has changed. He can sense movement in the painting. The mist drifts down. A puff of breeze starts at the far left, lifting and releasing a pine bough, and wafts across the painting, touching other pines here and there, its tendrils trailing through branches and subtly shifting the mist. It seems that he can see the forest breathing. The stream is seen to churn in places, and where the water's surface stands calm he glimpses the shadows of pine needles shimmering.

As the breeze drifts, he realizes it is the movement of the brush itself he is sensing – Li Wen's brush as it hovers over the painting and washes across it, spreading ink with all the subtlety and invisibility of a light breeze passing through a forest or furring a body of water.

The artist is standing on a trail at the foot of the mountain, a shape small and black as a burnt grain of rice. Donning the loupe goggles, the curator peers at the infinitesimal brushstrokes. Li Wen is pointing, while a fellow traveler stands next to him precisely at the spot where the waterfall becomes a stream, appearing and disappearing among bushes. *He must have found a friend along the way.* The curator checks the other paintings. *Yes, he now has a fellow traveller.*

Unlike the other paintings, here, the artist faces the viewer. Using the brush in his hand, he points the way along the trail ahead.

The curator reads aloud the line from Li Wen's summer poem. "*A powerful sun inhales the world.*"

He knows that Chinese paintings of the period were filled with secret codes of dissent and he wonders if this line might contain a hidden message. Every image in a painting could represent a political comment that would be discernible only to other artists and scholars. It was a way to air complaints among intellectuals who opposed the Court without being noticed by those in power. Everything was veiled, everything meant what it said – what it pictured – and something else.

He looks again. *The mountain represents the Emperor. It is so obviously at the centre of its world. And yet, at the bottom of the mountain, at its base, lies a thick banner of fog.* The curator leans back in his chair. *The mountain floats on nothing.*

∽

"Here. This way." Wen pointed with his walking stick, now worn and splintered from months of walking the mountains. The trail had led to a split and Wen chose the path on the right. His guess was correct. He possessed an uncanny ability to read the landscape and, like flowing water, find the most effortless way through. Wen, with his practiced eye could read his way through light and shadow, could find the thread that led them ever closer to the capital.

Five weeks later, Wen and Ming had passed through the final chain of mountains. Now all that separated them from the city of the Emperor, they were informed by peasants they met along the road, was a ten-day journey through rolling tea-hills. "Continue north-east," the peasants said, pointing, "always north-east. Ten days of walking. No more."

As the two friends descended a well-used track in the afternoon, they were sweaty with the mid-summer heat and humidity. Suddenly the sun disappeared behind a black cloud. Ming stopped, shaded his eyes and looked up. "Storm coming."

Masses of dark clouds were tumbling in from the west. "There's a hut down there. Hurry." The wind began to toss a line of distant willows and rip through the jade-green tea fields.

The two travellers trotted toward the hut at the bottom of the hillside trail, their packs bouncing. Nearing the hut, they saw that it was abandoned, the west-facing half of its thatched roof pocked with holes. They ducked through the open doorway just as the first fat drops spattered at their feet.

Inside, they shrugged out of their packs and collapsed onto straw piles under the part of the roof where less light penetrated. While they rested, the wind and rain came in earnest, blowing through the doorway and dripping from the shredded thatch. They edged into the only dry corner and waited.

Rain fell steadily for the rest of the afternoon and all evening. Throughout the night, lightning flared and flashed like skeletons of dragons in the sky. They managed to keep dry and by morning the storm had passed. Using bits of dry straw and sticks from inside the hut, Ming started a fire. After eating rice with a few wild greens, and drinking tea, they hoisted their packs and continued the journey.

Late the next day, they ambled along a path through the endless jade sea of tea fields stretching before them. Wen turned to look back the way they had come. Behind, in the clear, freshly-washed light, towered a massive cliff of bare stone. The great lone mountain stood higher and apart from the others, spattered here and there with small tufts of pine and spruce and mountain oak. He realized that he had found the scene for his fourth and final painting. To the left, a lively waterfall fell in white stitches, threading down through broken crags, stretching out into a stream in the lower reaches. Already the late-afternoon sun was setting behind the cliff.

"Let us find a place to camp. I have one last painting to accomplish before we gain the city."

Beside the stream, they spotted a glade of willows with dry protected ground nearby. There they camped and slept the night.

Wen awoke before dawn and lay gazing at the river of stars. It resembled his journey, this long hazy trail of the Milky Way. Lying on his back, he felt mist descending from the mountain and moistening his face. Light and delicate as the finest silk, the mist hardly seemed to exist at all, and yet, with its slow steady descent, it soaked the entire world.

The mountain thrust its wide granite spire up high into the clouds. Thinking of his final painting, Wen decided he would use vertical 'raindrop strokes' to achieve the effect of great height for the towering cliff.

The waterfall on the mountain appeared to tumble from the clouds themselves while, through the mist, the mountains in the distance resembled the faintly traced eyebrows of concubines.

At the same time, the base of the mountain itself was wrapped in thick fog. Already he was thinking of how he would paint the scene.

I live in a world of ink. It flows up the bole of every tree, through the complex of branches, out to the tip of each needle, along the fluted stems of every leaf, leaving faint cloudstains upon the sky like subtle patterns on silk. Ink flows up out of the earth and hardens into mountains, it rises as mist from crags and cracks, floats down from heaven as darkened clouds heavy with life. Each man walking a trail, each horse, each boat on the water is ink; the ink fishing line of the fisherman disappears into a lake of ink. He paused, gazed at the mountain again, simply looked at it without any thought. The words came to him unbidden: *The ink mountain floats on nothing.*

Later that morning, Ming decided to search out the local village for the day while Wen started on his final painting. After breakfast, Ming headed down a path through the tea fields and disappeared.

Wen gathered his brushes, inks and turtleshell inkstone. As before, he unrolled a blank sheet of paper and found stones to weigh down the corners. Checking the weather, he was pleased to find it turning into a fine day. The earlier tangle of cloud about the summit of the granite cliff had dissolved into sunlight. The morning dew as well had melted into the world, lending the slender willow leaves, the tea plantations and the surrounding hills a subtle sheen.

From his pack, he removed several dozen sketches he had made over the past few weeks, flicking through them to remind him of what was there. He chose the images of two willows that had caught his attention and that he considered placing near the bottom edge of the painting.

He held the brush of silk filaments over the blank page and contemplated the simple luminosity shining there. The image of the mountain as he had seen it in the mist of dawn arose simultaneously from his own depths and from the depths of the blank paper, like a diving kingfisher about to touch its own reflection on the surface of a lake.

Wen gripped the brush, the upturned turtle shell resting on the ground next to him. Without his noticing, a single drop of water had fallen from a nearly invisible cloud high above and landed directly in the shell.

In its descent from cloud to inkstone, the raindrop had captured the world in its watery mirror. The single wet pearl reflected a wealth of images: the towering cliff with its banners of pines, the silk-blue heavens, the near and distant landscape of peaks and mist. And if one were able to discern the infinite profundities of that single globe of water, one would see the entire Middle Kingdom itself stretching for thousands of *li* in every direction, and, in ever-diminishing subtleties, the rest of the world, known and unknown, the sun and moon, comets and stars.

When Wen took up his inkstone, he noted that it already contained a drop of water, its watery mirrors dissolved and alive. He scraped his ink stick along the inside of the shell, working up a small black tarn. Staring at his own reflection in the shimmering ink, he trusted that it already contained the painting within it.

He set to work. As his brush leapt and flew across the surface of the paper, he knew what the Emperor would see in the painting. The Emperor would recognize himself – the great mountain that stands alone, the heart and centre of all China, the middle point of the Middle Kingdom. The one towering presence that all subjects across the Empire look to for guidance and protection, and the one whose absolute power they most fear. *The Emperor will admire the way the cliff thrusts into the heavens. It will reaffirm that he is more than a man – he is a god, an immortal, the Son of Heaven, Emperor of China, the one called Huangdi, His Celestial Magnificence.*

Wen believed that the Emperor would be pleased to be presented in such a light, and the Emperor would ride his concubines that night with particular pleasure.

And yet Wen knew that he was not painting a symbol of the Emperor at all. He was simply painting a mountain, a mountain that stands on nothing.

Several days later, Ming started a fire to boil water and cook rice for breakfast. "Look. In the village, I found that they make tea in a different way here. This tea is called Dragon in the Clouds."

Wen stared down into Ming's palm. "Have the tea leaves been burnt?"

"Not quite. Roasted. Lightly scorched. They call it 'killing the green'. They do not steam their tea from green leaves, as we do, but roast it and brew it."

Ming tossed the tea into boiling water and removed the pot from the fire. A few moments later, he poured the mysterious tea into a cup. Wen tasted it and grimaced.

Ming laughed. "At first, I too did not like the flavour of this brewed tea, but in my short time in the village, the taste grew on me, and now I want nothing else. I hear it is all that they drink in the capital."

"I suspect they will do many things differently in the capital."

"When will we continue our journey? We have been here nearly a week."

"Soon. I have almost finished the final painting. A day or two more, that is all."

When Wen decided late the next day to brush a poem onto the completed painting of summer, he felt a sense of completion mixed with a feeling of emptiness. The feeling reminded him of those moments lying with the woman long ago, the wife of the cruel farmer, exhausted and emptied out from their lovemaking, and yet full and glowing with something else, something inexpressible.

As Wen took a sip of the unusual tea that Ming had brewed, he had a sudden inspiration for the poem. He swept up an ink stick and the turtleshell inkstone, added a bit of water and started grinding the stick. The words of the poem in his head were like feathers blown about in a strong wind. *He had the poem, he didn't have the poem.* It would appear and disappear, like a bird passing through a forest, stitching among the trees. He kept grinding, trying to hold onto the inspiration, the first flash of the poem, the incredibly evanescent words. A hooded pitta called from the next hill, a fluty trilling. Wen looked up as the pitta dropped from the branch and flew off. He finished grinding the ink, realizing that the bird had taken the poem with it. He sat, waiting for it to come back. It was gone.

The next morning, when he awoke, the poem returned, not quite the same but close enough. Again he ground ink and, when ready, took up his calligraphy brush and wrote the poem on the painting.

> Mist descends from the clouds
> Breathes from a mountain's deep crags
>
> The needles of pines drip with moisture
> Rocks reveal wet stains that resemble granite peaks
>
> Nothing escapes the touch of mist
> Without hurry it penetrates everywhere soaks everything
>
> Then rising above the cliff on a summer morning
> A powerful sun inhales the world

~

The travellers spent the next seven days traversing the tea-growing district, a landscape of smooth rolling hills, followed by a region of muddy rice paddies and countless small lakes. After working their way across this rice-growing district, Li Wen and Ming finally approached West Lake, which marked the western edge of the capital, Linan.

With growing excitement they arrived at the lake late in the day, their afternoon shadows anxious to enter the city ahead of them. Around the long lake edged with old twisted willows they could see pavilions of dazzling gold and blue, and a lofty pagoda to the south. Here and there, under the trees, peddlers sold fruit or drinks or cooked food.

In the distance, the two travellers glimpsed the city reflected on the water. Ten thousand roofs sparkled, their tiles overlapping like fish-scales. They smelled the city faintly on the air, snatches of cooking scents and human waste. And they could hear a subtle distant buzz. They decided to stay the night by the lake and enter the city in the morning.

Lying with his head resting on a grass tussock, Wen stared up at the stars. Ming too was awake and gave voice to his thoughts. "Perhaps we should consider turning back tomorrow. Perhaps we should return now to the mountains, before it is too late."

"Why do you say this, Ming, after we have come all this way?"

"I long to see my native town again, my family."

"There is no shame in that. Do you wish to return to your family home, to your ancestors, now, before we enter the city?"

"Perhaps. I don't know. I do not know what to expect."

"You are free to do as you wish, my friend. You are welcome to come with me or to return home. It is up to you, though I would miss you beyond measure. As for me, I am bound to complete my task and deliver the message and the long-life paintings to the Emperor, as I have promised."

"I fear the city. So many thousands of people with strange ways. I am a simple peasant."

"Yes, your fears are not unfounded. The capital will be far different than Jinhan. It will be both marvellous and frightening, I am sure. We will no doubt see inconceivable things. Temptations, and beauty, beyond belief. Much suffering too, much sorrow." Wen sensed, that if it were not for Ming's simple, powerful sense of loyalty, he would turn for home in the morning without ever seeing the capital or the Emperor.

"Will you ever see your paintings again, once you have presented your gift?"

"Perhaps they will be put on display in the Court. Or perhaps not. I don't know."

"But surely, if you want to see them, it will be allowed?"

Wen found the discussion taking an odd turn. "It is possible they will be placed in the Court's Inner Storage, only to be seen by the eyes of the Emperor, his closest aides and his concubines. They are a gift; once given, it is up to the Emperor how to deal with them. Why do you ask?"

Ming paused, ignoring the question, and then spoke as if he had made a difficult decision. "Just as you have promised to deliver the paintings to the Emperor, I too have made a promise – to come with you to the capital."

Late that night, Ming stayed awake while Wen's heavy snores revealed that he had drifted into deep sleep. Lighting a faggot in the dying fire, Ming planted it in the ground behind a row of bushes that kept him hidden from Wen's view should he wake. He opened Wen's pack and extracted the paintings of spring and summer from the bamboo tube. Holding them carefully under the flame tugging in the soft nightime breeze, he played each of the works through his hands, concentrating on the changes in the landscape and the order in which they appeared. He committed the entire journey to memory, exactly as he had traveled it: a single line ran from Jinhan to the tomb where they had been imprisoned, across the dry lands, over rivers and mountains, rice paddies and tea hills, all of which Li Wen had placed in the paintings.

Again he concentrated on the painting of spring. He wanted to ensure he would be able to find the tomb again, that he would not forget the way, for he knew that once he found the tomb, the town of his ancestors was not many days off. *The paintings will surely be safe for a long time. No one would dare destroy a gift to the Emperor*, he encouraged himself. *Yet, this may be the last time I can study them. I must put this map clearly into my memory tonight. Each detail. Each curve in the trail, each mountain and river. I must remember the tallest pines, the location of Mount Tung, where the monasteries and inns are located, the paths through tea plantations and rice paddies.*

For hours, until just before dawn, he sat studying the paintings, concentrating on their details. Like many who do not have the gift of the written word, he had instead a prodigious memory.

Finally, the first embers of dawn shimmered on the horizon. Ming re-rolled the two paintings and worked them back inside the bamboo tube, which he returned to Wen's pack.

空虚
[Emptiness]

The Hall of Pure Emptiness

THE CURATOR OF CHINESE ART wanders through the spring landscape. He smells the incense of the forest on the mountain slopes. He turns from the painting and glances out the window that looks over the park. It is early evening. The shadows under the oaks in the park are deepening while the concrete and glass towers surrounding the park are set ablaze by the setting sun.

He sits back a moment in his chair. *Sometimes I feel I am simply an eye, a disembodied eye inside my jeweler's loupe, journeying across the landscape, on and on. At other times, I'm inside the painting itself. I feel my hand on top of the artist's as the brush sweeps down and across the page, as if I'm in the landscape while painting it.*

The curator senses someone at his door but when he turns to look, no one is there. As he returns to watching Li Wen walk the trail, the curator wonders if someone, in another time, another place, is watching him.

Thus it was that on the first day of the seventh lunar month, in the ninth year of the reign of Emperor Duzong, 15th emperor of the Song dynasty, in the Year of the Water Rooster, Wen and Ming hiked around West Lake, crossed over an arched stone bridge and entered the city of Linan through one of its thirteen towering gates. Beside the gate, groups of men lounged and visited. They stared at the two strangers as they entered.

From the gate, a wide, brick-paved thoroughfare led into the city. Wen and especially Ming were intimidated by the crowds:

two-wheeled carts loaded with vegetables were pulled by farmers, soldiers muscled past in groups, children shot everywhere underfoot, their heads shaved but for a small tuft of hair on top. A thin dusty man passed leading a mule laden with pots, and two other burly workers jostled the travellers as they hurried by carrying over their shoulders bamboo poles from which hung swaying baskets. Ming stood staring and was nearly run down by a carriage with curtained windows carried by four strong porters. As he leapt out of harm's way, a man on horseback shouted at him to watch out or he would be trampled. From every corner, food peddlers cried out, trying to attract customers.

In front of them, a lady's palanquin with red silk curtains parted the crowd and came to a halt. The commoners nearby stood back and waited. The lady stepped down into the road, and with the help of two women servants, took tiny steps on bound feet the size of an infant's and passed through a decorated gate into a building.

Ming, dizzy from the heat of a summer morning, the rank city smells and the crowds, turned to Wen. "Where will we go? How will you be able to gain an audience with the Emperor?"

"My master has given me the name of a scholar-official, an old friend of his. He promised that this man will help us gain entrance to the Imperial Court."

For the rest of the day, the travellers wandered through the streets of the great city, crossing dozens of narrow, hump-backed bridges that spanned a network of canals. They passed rows of double-story houses and workshops, immense rice granaries and armouries. In the most crowded areas, Wen and Ming walked shoulder to shoulder with strangers, everyone jostling, everyone in a hurry. Like Wen and Ming, the commoners were dressed in hempen clothes, sandals of hemp on their feet. Hawkers shouted and beat sheets of metal for attention. Artisans bowed over worktables on the ground floors of houses, while the congested streets bustled with entertainers and prostitutes.

The city was scattered throughout with high towers. "For the sighting of fires," a fish peddler told them. "If you see a flag on top of a tower, run to West Lake."

Wen and Ming bought a bowl of congee with silver ginkgo nuts and a silkworm pie and shared them while sitting in the dust and leaning against a wall.

Ming leaned over his food and stared at the ground while he chewed.

"What is it, Ming? Is something wrong?"

"It is overwhelming, this city. The noise, so many strange people."

"You will get used to it, I'm sure. Are you enjoying the food?"

"Yes, very much."

Having finished their meal, they continued their wandering, passing innumerable shops selling salted fish, rice, offal, ten-pound pears, yellow and white peaches. Along broad avenues more than forty paces wide, they passed rows of taverns with flags hanging limp in the heat. Ming kept stopping to stare at the marvels in the luxurious shops: beauty products for ladies, crickets in cages, live cats and fish, chessmen, oiled paper for windows. Along the street, ladies paraded by, followed by their servants holding parasols. A woman passed them, wearing her hair pulled back into a chignon decorated with an ivory comb and sparkling jewellery.

Ming turned and stared at her.

"What is it, Ming? Why do you stare?"

"I have never seen such beautiful women. The women in my town are not like this."

"You prefer the women of your own town?"

"I am a simple-minded peasant. What would I do with a woman like that?"

Wen noticed a teahouse where scholars and officials in purple robes were passing in and out. Upon entering the teahouse, the two travellers were invited to wash their hands in a bowl by the entrance and were seated at a table by a young hostess. The two travellers gazed about.

"It is very beautiful, this teahouse," commented Wen. Dwarf evergreens stood in decorated porcelain pots, paintings of red and green dragons adorned the walls, lanterns of crimson paper hung in rows. In shadowy booths, singing girls entertained gentlemen and sipped tiny cups of plum-flower or rice wine.

Ming stared at a girl in one of the booths across the room, a quizzical look on his face. "Are they prostitutes?" he asked

"I suspect so," said Wen.

An elegant young woman with a phoenix comb in her hair served Wen and Ming brewed tea in porcelain cups carried on a lacquered tray. Ming kept his eyes down, too embarrassed to look at the serving girl or the wealthy patrons. Again sensing his discomfort, Wen leaned forward and explained. "I am hoping that perhaps someone in this establishment will know the whereabouts of Yang Su, the scholar-official we seek. Please, Ming, enjoy your tea."

An elderly scholar glided past their table, a young attendant following behind holding a parasol of blue-green silk. Floor-length robes of silver lace over dark red marked the scholar as a sixth rank official. Wen, bowing, addressed him. "Sir, most benevolent lord, a question."

The scholar-official paused, his hands coming out from his robe's wide sleeves and crossing in polite greeting. "Yes?" He sniffed the air and Wen was sure that the scholar found the smell of these two coarse strangers distasteful. Wen noted that the scholar exuded the scent of chrysanthemums.

"My lord, do you perhaps know of an official named Yang Su?"

"I do. The distinguished scholar and minister Yang Su is well known. Why do you ask?"

"We carry a message for him from an old friend. Can you tell me where we can find him?"

"Of course." He turned and pointed. "Follow this road to the south end of the city. He can be found in an area called the Hill of Ten Thousand Pines near the Imperial Palace. That is where many high officials live. His residence is called the Hall of Pure Emptiness."

After thanking the man, Wen paid and they left the teahouse, heading in the direction the scholar had indicated. Feeling uneasy, Wen wondered what such a lofty scholar as Yang Su would make of these two rustic characters.

Not far from the tavern and teahouse area, they passed an alcohol storage facility guarded by soldiers. Wen asked one of the soldiers for directions to the Hill of Ten Thousand Pines. The soldier tilted his head and narrowed his gaze. "What business have you there?"

"I carry a message for the distinguished scholar, Yang Su."

"You had best visit the baths before heading to the area where the officials live. If you want my advice, looking as you do, you won't get an audience with Yang Su or anyone else." He turned and pointed. "Just before this road comes to the Imperial Way, you will see a sign with a pot on it over the door. As today is a day of the Rat, few will be bathing so you should have no trouble finding space."

Wen and Ming thanked him and walked on, soon arriving at the public baths. A peddler at the doorway sold them hot water and liquid soap made of peas and herbs. Wen paid the fee for the baths and they entered.

Although the spacious bath could have accommodated a hundred men, the place was more than half-empty, as the soldier had predicted. Wen and Ming quickly undressed and submerged themselves with a gasp in the frigid water.

An hour later, freshly washed and newly shaved, they were climbing the Hill of Ten Thousand Pines, enquiring of passers-by the way to the residence of Yang Su. After several wrong turns, they entered an area of wealthy pavilions surrounded by spacious gardens. Eventually, they approached a gate that indicated it was the entrance to the Hall of Pure Emptiness. Flanking the entrance were painted images of the traditional gate gods, meant to keep away demons and evil influences. Beyond the gate, they glimpsed a midsummer garden bursting with lush vegetation: cassia trees, orchids, chrysanthemums, tall ginkgos, and clusters of willow and bamboo. The air smelled sweet and flowery. On their arrival, a servant scurried to the gate and swung it open. A ginger cat slipped out and curled around Ming's ankle in greeting.

"We seek an audience with the distinguished scholar, Yang Su. I am the painter Li Wen."

The servant scrunched up his face. "Who?"

From the porch of the pavilion with its upturned roof, the two travellers noticed a tall man in sea-green robes regarding them with interest.

"My master in the south, Fu Wei, would like to send his greetings to Yang Su, his old friend and colleague."

Before the servant could turn them away, Yang Su boomed from the porch: "Let them in."

Wen and Ming, on seeing the master of the house approach, immediately fell to the ground, kowtowing on the threshold of the gate.

~

In the gardens surrounding the house of Yang Su, red-breasted parakeets chirped from the branches of a cassia tree. Yang Su, in his green silk robes, sat across from Li Wen and Ming. All three relaxed on low chairs with high backs, a table of dark wood between them where cups of tea and a teapot of fine pale green celadon rested. Yang Su exuded the fragrance of crushed orchids.

Ming had never before entered a household of such luxury. Fine red nets stretched across the windows to keep out insects, and outside, in the gardens, jades chimed in the breeze.

Yang Su spoke. "Lady Yang sends her regrets. She had hoped to join us for tea as she is anxious to meet you both. But she is not feeling well today."

"I am sorry to hear that," Wen said.

"Master, are you a man of the Way, a Buddhist monk?" Ming asked the scholar, indicating his hairless head.

"No, no," Yang Su chuckled. "I have been bald for many years. Hair will not stick to my head."

Wen ran his fingers through his own hair. "No place for the lice to live then."

"True, true. It has its advantages."

They sipped from their cups of tea, the new brewed style common to the capital. Wen immediately liked Yang Su. For a scholar and an official of vast power, he was not at all pretentious and treated his guests with warmth and respect.

"This tea, where does it come from?" Wen asked.

"From the hills of the region. The farmers call it Forest of Fragrance tea. Not quite as fine as Dragon Well tea, which is reserved for the imperial household alone. The farmers who grow Forest of Fragrance use soy-bean cakes for fertilizer and gather it during the fifth solar term when new twigs have just begun to grow. They pick only two leaves and a bud per plant. Do you enjoy it?"

Wen nodded. "We have nothing like it in the South." He guessed that Yang Su was slightly younger than One Tooth. Not yet an old man, but well past his prime. Wen asked: "How is it you knew One Tooth, or Fu Wei, as you probably remember him?"

"Ah, yes, One Tooth. I had forgotten Fu Wei's style name." He gazed out into the garden. "It was long ago that Fu Wei left us. He was a Director in the Ministry of Rites then – an important position for one so young. He had performed admirably in the exams, and was considered one of the highest-ranking scholars in the capital. But then …" He paused, thinking. "It was all so long ago. I don't think I knew even then exactly what had happened, although there were more rumours than grains of rice in the Imperial granaries. The present Emperor's uncle, Lizong, was Emperor at the time. Fu Wei had a falling out with a powerful official who turned the Emperor against him. Like many great men before and since, he was sent into exile in the far south. I am surprised to hear he has not succumbed to the fevers and other illnesses that abound in those pestilential climes. Did he ever speak of his life here in the capital?"

"Fu Wei never spoke of it, never mentioned wanting to return. He seemed quite content living in the south. Soon after he arrived there, he became a monk and is now the abbot of a small but prosperous monastery. I doubt he would leave."

Still, Wen suddenly wondered if he had been wrong all along about the message he was carrying from Fu Wei for the Emperor. *Perhaps the message caught in that narrow bamboo throat concerns One Tooth attempting to have his exile rescinded.* Wen suddenly recalled a visitor to Fu Wei from the capital who had arrived at the monastery several months before Wen himself had started his journey. The visitor had spent hours in conversation with the master about conditions at the Court. *Perhaps the gift of the paintings to the present Emperor is meant to help ease Fu Wei's return.*

A servant came in and filled their cups from the teapot.

Ming asked Yang Su: "What is your position in the Court, Master?"

"I am Director of the Imperial Library."

"You must have many important duties."

"Yes, it is a great honour to serve the Emperor in this capacity. However, I am well aware that imperial favour can disappear overnight, as I have seen happen too often in the past. I have been fortunate to survive the ups and downs of politics for all these years."

There was a silent pause while they sipped their tea. Placing his cup back down on the table, Wen said, "There is something I must ask of you. I feel ashamed even to ask such a favour, to prevail upon your good graces, but it is my duty to do so. I bear a message that Fu Wei has given me for the Emperor. And a long-life gift as well, consisting of four landscapes that Fu Wei asked me to paint during my journey here. Can you help me to gain an audience in order to deliver them to the Emperor, along with Fu Wei's best wishes?"

Su rubbed his chin a moment and gave thought to precisely what had been on Wen's mind. "Perhaps Fu Wei seeks an end to his exile and a return to the capital? I wonder. I am convinced our present Emperor would welcome him."

"I am unaware of Fu Wei's intentions, for I have been forbidden to read the message I carry and my master gave no indication as to its content. I was instructed to deliver it personally to the Emperor. Will it be possible for you to arrange an audience?"

"I believe that the Emperor will be pleased to hear from Fu Wei. My old friend One Tooth was the Emperor's tutor when the Son of Heaven was a child. As I recall, our Emperor Duzong has fond memories of Fu Wei from that period of his life."

Wen startled. "Oh. I had no idea One Tooth was once the Emperor's tutor."

"Yes. They were as close as older brother and younger. This surprises you?"

"It does. My master never mentioned it."

"If I recall my old friend, he was one who never said more than was absolutely necessary."

Wen wondered again what could possibly be in the message he was bearing. For the first time, he feared the moment he would be standing before the throne while the Emperor read through the message. *It could contain anything. If nothing else, the master was always unpredictable, seemed to revel in his unpredictability. I will feel completely exposed and unable to defend myself. I hope my tongue does not turn to lead if I am asked by the Emperor to respond.*

Su interrupted Wen's thoughts. "I trust an audience with the Emperor can be arranged, but it will take time."

"Yes, I understand."

"In the meantime, you and Ming are my welcome guests. For as long as you remain in the capital, you may call the Hall of Pure Emptiness your home. Come, I will show you to your sleeping quarters and after you rest, we will eat."

Yang Su led them through a series of rooms and courtyards, including a moon-viewing porch and a library. These were followed by music and banquet pavilions. When they entered a courtyard surrounded by pines with low hanging boughs pruned to maximize shade, Su explained, "This is where we rest on the hottest evenings." The air was thick with the fragrance of a deep evergreen forest.

To the east of the main room of the house, Yang Su paused and bowed in the ancestral hall, which contained an altar holding the spirit tablets of his ancestors. Except in the servants' quarters, the floors throughout the residence were paved with glazed bricks, and those in the courtyards had water running under them, helping to further cool those areas.

As they settled into their room, Wen placing his pack in a corner and Ming testing the bed, Wen asked. "So, what do you think, Ming?"

"This is a most comfortable house. I have not slept in a bed in many months. But what about you? When Su mentioned your master and his relationship with the Emperor, your face became clouded. It was a look I have not seen from you before, ever."

"I was surprised. My master had told me little about his time in the capital. I was startled to hear he had been so close to the Emperor."

"Do you fear this audience with His Majesty?"

"I do not know what to expect. I am certainly uneasy about it. And you?"

"Terrified. I will only come because I promised you I would."

Through the night, the sound of a distant drum announcing the hours punctuated Wen's sleep. In the morning, he awoke to the clamour of young monks using fish-shaped wooden clackers to herald the dawn. "Cloudy day, cloudy day," the monks chanted the weather report. Later, Wen and Ming saw these same monks holding out their bowls and begging for alms.

On his third day as a guest at the house, while Ming was helping a servant remove a fallen tree near the gate, Wen was reading in the garden in the quiet of afternoon. Yang Su approached him. Su had just come from official duties, his seal of office affixed to the sash of his robe, tied by the red cord reserved for esteemed members of the government.

Sunlight and shade dappled Yang Su's long robe as he stood before Wen, a scattering of fallen black blossoms at his feet. Su bowed. "Forgive me for interrupting your contemplations. I wish to let you know that I have invited an important guest from the Court to join us this evening for a feast."

Wen held open in his lap a book of poems by Tu Fu. The book was decorated with shadows of slit, double-lobed ginkgo leaves. He looked up and smiled. "Yes? Who is it?"

"Our eminent guest is Po Cheng, Director of the Imperial Academy of Painting and one of China's greatest flower artists. He is especially skilled at painting orchids. His work is extraordinary. Certain of his paintings are so precise one can tell the time of day by the light falling on the blossoms. Quite astonishing. Po also happens to be Head of the Palace Eunuchs and a favourite of the Emperor. The Emperor considers his opinion in all important matters. The eunuch has amassed considerable wealth from the rental of warehouses he owns in the north end of the city."

"I look forward to meeting him. Will Lady Yang be joining us?"

"No, I am afraid not." Yang Su paused. "How can I say this delicately? She finds it difficult to be in Po Cheng's presence. She would prefer not to spend time with him. Also, since Ming is your servant, I will leave it up to you to decide if he shall join us or take his meal with the servants of the household."

"My apologies – Ming is not my servant but my travel companion. It is my wish that he join us."

"So be it." Changing the subject, Yang Su asked, "If you don't mind my asking, Wen, what is your style name?"

"I do not mind in the least. I was given my style name by Fu Wei who suggested the name Ink Mountain."

"Ah, an intriguing name for an artist. Perhaps this evening, after our feast, you will be willing to show us the paintings you have brought for the Emperor. I look forward to seeing them as will Po

Cheng, I am sure. Until then, I will leave you to your reading. I have much work to do this afternoon. Farewell."

When Yang Su left, Wen decided to take a stroll through the gardens. The residence of Yang Su was half-hidden in the midst of spacious, well-kept grounds. Wen walked along beside the smooth flow of a narrow stream. He noticed Ming, his work with the servants finished, seated by a shallow waterfall, with his back to Wen, staring down at something in his fingers. Wen approached. Ming heard his footsteps and turned.

"Have you seen the silver fish in the pools?" Ming asked, slipping the coin into his pocket. Not quickly enough, for the movement caught Wen's attention. He noticed the flash of gold, but said nothing.

"They are known as long-life fishes. Do you not recall, we saw them being raised in ponds outside the west gates when we first arrived."

"Yes, I remember."

Wen considered the stream and the delicate knee-high waterfall. "With these craggy stones, and the dwarf trees planted about, this spot seems a miniature version of one of the mountain sites we passed earlier in the summer."

Ming too glanced about. "It reminds me of one of your paintings."

"I believe it is meant to replicate the atmosphere of those high forests, the peace one finds there."

"I have never seen such a place as this garden. It is like a dream."

"I agree. This entire city is like a dream."

In the cool of early evening, when the sun had started to descend and the starkest heat of day was passing, a servant led Wen and Ming to the banquet pavilion. As Wen entered the room, Yang Su turned and greeted him. "Wen, I would like to introduce you to Po Cheng, Director of the Imperial Academy of Painting."

The two men bowed to each other. The eunuch, dressed in robes of purple silk, gazed out steadily from under hooded eyes. His head was hairless, his lips fleshy and pale, the corners of his mouth turned down. He was slightly younger than Wen but his eyes had something old about them, an exhausted worldliness.

"Our esteemed host tells me you are a painter." Po Cheng's voice was dry, uninspired. Wen noted the small, soft-looking hands. "I did not know there were painters in the south."

"There are painters throughout the Middle Kingdom. The south is no different."

The eunuch leaned to the side. "And who is that cowering behind you?"

Yang Su spoke up. "This is Ming. Wen's travelling companion."

Po Cheng looked him up and down. "He looks like a peasant." The eunuch turned to Wen and added, "I am anxious to view your paintings, to learn what a man from the south can do with brush and ink."

"But first, we will eat," Yang Su announced.

The four men sat on high-backed wooden chairs around a table covered in a crimson cloth and set with chopsticks and spoons. Yang Su motioned for the servers to begin. Cups of rice wine were poured and a steady line of servants carried in lacquer trays filled with small porcelain bowls. Pimiento soup with mussels and goose with peaches and apricots were followed by shrimps cooked in rice-wine. Small pieces of roebuck were served in delicate green bowls thin as chrysanthemum leaves.

"What is this?" Wen asked his host, pointing into a bowl with his chopstick.

Yang Su looked. "White fish cooked with plums, and those are snails."

The discussion revolved around the food and the eight kinds of rice wine that were served with the various courses through the evening. The conversation was limited to three of the diners, Ming remaining silent throughout, his head bowed to his bowl as he ate. Po Cheng offered his opinion on his first sip of each wine that was served, without a care as to what his host thought of his comments. "Ambrosia," he gushed, followed by "no better than dog urine" or "infected with sea water" or "elegant in the extreme, yes, yes, most elegant."

Meanwhile, Wen and Ming were overwhelmed by the richness of the exotic food after their months of simple fare in the mountains. Steamed baby pig in garlic was followed by pork cheeks. Fried sparrow gizzards were served along with whole duck heads, the skulls removed, making it easier to suck out the brains and retrieve the delicate tongues.

Wen was spinning. He began to limit himself to minute sips from his wine. Meanwhile, Po Cheng and Yang Su continued to down full cups as soon as they were served.

A piece of duck dangling from his chopsticks, the eunuch claimed, "It is said that the people of the island of Hainan eat flies and worms. Is this true as well in other areas of the south?"

"Never," Wen said. "No one in Hainan or elsewhere in the south eats flies and worms."

"I also hear that the people of the south eat snake and grasshoppers, calling them 'brushwood eels' and 'brushwood shrimp'; and they consume rats, which they refer to as 'household deer'. Is it so?"

Wen twirled his cup. "You have many wrong notions about the south, I am afraid. We are not barbarians."

"Let me ask our peasant." The eunuch turned and, smiling, looked straight at Ming who tucked his chin into his chest under the direct gaze. "Tell me, what is your favourite food?"

Ming looked at Wen and hesitated. He began to breathe heavily and turned back to the eunuch. "My favourite of all foods?"

"Yes, yes; that which you favour the most."

Yang Su, a little drunk as well, spoke up. "Be honest now, Ming. Of all the foods of the south, which do you favour?"

Ming mumbled something.

The eunuch leaned forward. "What is that? Speak up. Come, come. Tell us, peasant. Out with it."

Ming, embarrassed, offered a muffled response. "Blood and offal soup."

The eunuch threw his head back and cackled. Yang Su had the politeness to stifle his laugh with his hand.

A moment later, Po Cheng asked Wen, "Are you a monk? You don't look or dress like one but perhaps they do things differently in the south."

Wen swallowed. "No; I am a lay practitioner of Buddhism, a simple painter."

"Have you a wife, a family?"

"No."

"I trust you are aware that the Buddhists are out of favour at Court? I myself could never see much sense in their rituals and meditations. This mixing of our Confucian beliefs with the ways of the Indian sage is a dangerous mistake."

This was followed by a long silence in which all present continued to eat and drink.

I am glad he has not asked if I agree with him, Wen thought, chewing on a sweet pork dumpling. *Yang Su appears to be ignoring him. Perhaps he has heard it all before.*

Later, a gloomier atmosphere penetrated the room with the lateness of the hour. The talk switched to the ongoing battles in the north.

"What do you hear from the borders? Will our armies continue to hold the Mongols back?" Yang Su asked the eunuch, who was privy to the rumours that circulated ceaselessly like invisible winds through the Court.

Suddenly sober, the eunuch paused and glanced sharply at Yang Su. "It does not look favourable. Our generals are weak and utterly incompetent. As you know, the city of Xiangyang has been under siege for over a year. If the city capitulates, the Yangtze River will be lost to the Mongols and I fear Linan itself could follow.

Last week, news came of another failed attempt to break out of the besieged city. Two thousand of our men lost – beheaded by the enemy, their heads displayed on stakes for the benefit of those still within the walls. We have over ten thousand troops trapped there who can do nothing. Luckily, they say there is ten years' worth of grain in the city to sustain them. But, as I hear it, the enemy stays out of range of our crossbows."

The eunuch downed another cup. "I believe it is the end of times, the end of civilization. To be overwhelmed by these *barbarians...*," he spat. "They do not even recognize the name of Confucius. I thought perhaps when their leader, Möngke Khan, died that we would be able to escape this scourge, but the new Khan – they call him Kublai – appears more than capable of continuing the onslaught."

Wen spoke up. "But, I have heard that Linan will remain safe, as it is surrounded by lakes and rice paddies where horse armies cannot easily pass. Do not the Mongols travel only by horse and is that not their fatal weakness?"

Po shrugged. "That is the belief of many. We shall see. I myself have suggested numerous times that we need to increase the numbers of our horse soldiers but I am vehemently opposed by others in the Court."

Yang Su said. "It is First Minister Jia Sidao who opposes you, is it not? His hatred for you is well known."

"Yes." The eunuch paused, staring at the cup he held in his hand. "Perhaps one day, we shall all be exiled to the south. In any case, I am told by the 'gentlemen of the yellow carriage', those who collect hearsay from commoners," he explained for Wen's benefit, "that the people are losing faith in our generals, and even in the Emperor himself."

Yang Su shook his head. "*One by one the stars go out,*" he said, quoting a famous poem by Tang poet, Tu Fu, and added, "Our universe is out of harmony. What does the Son of Heaven say about this?"

Po Cheng again turned a cup of wine in his fingers while considering the question. "Not one of these words leaves this room. Do you understand me?" he said to the two visitors and then continued, "Emperor Duzong relies on First Minister Jia Sidao for all decisions concerning military affairs. I must say, the Emperor has never shown the least expertise in judging the quality of horses."

Wen recognized the expression. It was a way for Po Cheng to say that the Emperor lacked the ability to judge men. *And what does it say about your own favour in the court?* Wen pondered, thinking of the eunuch himself.

Po continued. "What I have long feared is coming to pass. The Emperor relies too much on First Minister Jia. Meanwhile, the Emperor's main interests are drink and his concubines. Entire villages have been emptied to service his needs. His sexual appetite is voracious and he neglects his duties entirely. Though the people still believe their Emperor is the Son of Heaven, some now say that he will be struck down as retribution for his lack of filial piety."

Wen and Ming were astounded to hear the Emperor spoken of in such a way.

Wen was also shocked to realize that events in the capital had come to such a pass. To think that the Emperor had failed in his duties made Wen feel as if he were falling, no floor, no ground, beneath him. Glancing at Ming, he noticed that his friend too felt this. Ming appeared like a frightened child, a stunned look on his face.

The eunuch continued. "You must understand that Jia Sidao is a most cruel man who trusts no one. When one of the Emperor's concubines informed Duzong that Xiangyang had been under siege for over a year – a simple truth that had been kept from the Son of Heaven – the Minister had her murdered for providing this information which might upset the Emperor. When another of the Emperor's concubines remarked on the beauty of a young man she spotted on the bank of West Lake, the Minister arranged to have the poor fellow executed in her presence."

Yang Su spoke up. "I hear the Emperor has become obsessed

with gaining immortality. Each morning no order of business can be addressed until he drinks from a bowl of dew collected in the four corners of the Imperial Gardens. He believes that dew is the drink favoured by the immortals."

"That is not all," the eunuch continued. "In his obsession with immortality, every day he eats powdered jade, quicksilver and various fungi. Worst of all are the Emperor's delusions. He insists that his armies will reconquer our capital city in the north. This is absurd. Our army is weak. Many of our soldiers are only in the army as punishment for crimes they have committed."

Yang Su said, "But what of the scholars? Can we not together do something to gain the Emperor's attention and remedy this situation?"

The eunuch sighed. "The scholars. What have they done? No fault of yours for I know you have warned against the worst offences, but it appears to have no effect. The court scholars waste their time on useless rituals and formality. There are now fifteen hundred volumes of rules for the formal reception of tributary envoys from Korea. Fifteen hundred! Another twelve hundred volumes of rules govern the emperor's ritual use of the Imperial Hall of Light. This is where the scholars have brought us."

Yang Su shook his head. "Confucius has said that one of the requirements of government is that the people have confidence in their ruler." He paused. Nothing more needed to be said for all to gather his meaning. "But enough somber talk of these dark times," Yang Su continued. "Tell us of your travels, Wen. You must have seen many wonders."

Before Wen could speak, an excited, drunken Ming blurted out, "Tell them of the tomb with the gol..." but he stopped in mid-sentence, silenced by a severe look from Wen.

"A tomb?" the eunuch inquired.

"It was nothing," Wen replied. But he knew that the eunuch had noticed the sharp glance he used to silence Ming.

"I see," Po Cheng said, not pressing the issue for the moment.

A servant came to the door, stepped into the room and whispered to Yang Su who then suggested they retire to the music room where he had arranged for a singing girl to play the pipa for their entertainment. When they rose, Ming stumbled and bumped into Wen who held him by the shoulders to straighten him up. A disturbed look flushed Ming's face and he turned, hurried to the doorway, leaned over the porch and vomited noisily into the chrysanthemums below. Po Cheng grinned, shaking his head as the three men retired to the music room. Ming followed sheepishly, beads of sweat pearling on his forehead.

In the music room, a young woman with tiny bound feet, painted eyebrows and a butterfly-shaped mouth stood when they entered. With a deep bow, she offered them comfortable low seats. As she raised a silk fan to hide her lips, Wen was drawn to her elegant long fingers. Her beauty was almost dangerously fragile, like a blossom whose petals would crumble at a touch. Her cheek was marked with a faint quarter-moon tattoo and her ink-black hair was gathered in a chignon and decorated with an elaborate silver dragon comb. Kneeling down, she leaned over slowly to place her fan aside on a low table. A moment later, when she strummed the large, four-stringed pipa and began her song, Wen thought her throat resembled the stem of an orchid that blossoms over and over with the flower of a melodious voice. He closed his eyes and floated away.

The penultimate song she played that evening was one known as *White Snow*, a tune that was thousands of years old. Li Wen turned to his host and whispered. "I know this tune from my childhood. It is said that whenever it is played, the gods, drawn by the beauty of its melody, descend to earth to listen."

At the end, the woman played the ancient classic, *Spring on a Moonlit River*. Wen relaxed into its introspective, quiet notes and when he opened his eyes again, a sliver of pure silvery white moon had appeared over the garden. Perhaps too quickly he took it as an auspicious sign. Yang Su stood. "Let us now see your paintings, Wen. It is time. I, for one, can wait no longer."

"Of course. Ming, would you gather a few small stones from the garden." Ming, his head hanging low, nodded without looking up, and made his way out. Meanwhile, Li Wen went to his room to fetch the paintings.

Returning to the music pavilion, Wen removed the four paintings from the bamboo tube, set them out with the stones Ming had gathered to weigh down the corners and stood back. Po Cheng approached, Wen observing him from the corner of his eye. Wen was practiced at determining what people truly felt about his work, despite what they might say. He surreptitiously contemplated the eunuch's face, and noted that Po Cheng was unable to hide his shock. *He did not expect work of this quality,* Wen thought. *The eunuch appears surprised, perhaps jealous, but I have no doubt he will hide his envy with skill.*

After lingering before each of the four paintings, Yang Su spoke. "These are astonishing. Landscapes of utter purity and harmony. I have never in my life seen such fine brushwork. The lines are fluid and smooth as one would expect of great painting. The Emperor will be well pleased with his long-life gift, very pleased, I am sure."

The others waited to hear what Po Cheng would say. The eunuch continued passing back and forth before the paintings, without speaking. Finally, he paused and sighed. "The four seasons are well represented. They are credible landscapes. But today, the finest painters work in more up-to-date realistic modes. There is much to be revealed in a simple bird, a single orchid. I and my fellow academicians believe in 'life painting', the pure expression of elegance, whereas it is clear that you follow a more traditional school, in which an elevated grandeur or magnificence is primary. Nevertheless, I suppose the Emperor will find them of interest."

While Yang Su was taken aback, the eunuch's reaction was exactly as Wen had expected. "Come, come," the host urged his friend to reconsider. "Are they not some of the finest landscapes you have seen? They fairly vibrate with harmony and balance."

Li Wen said quietly, "I follow no school. I simply paint what I see and feel."

The eunuch continued. "They are reasonable landscapes, as I said. Dynamic and harmonious, I cannot deny. Fine brushwork and composition, without a doubt. Well painted altogether, but in what I would call an antique mode. Today's leading artists have other interests, I am afraid. Other subjects. There is no doubt that these paintings are from the provinces, from a somewhat talented amateur who is distant from the heart of things."

Yang Su attempted again to come to Wen's defense: "Bird and flower paintings too have been done since ancient times. There is nothing new about those subjects."

Po Cheng nodded. "It is true. The subjects existed in antiquity. It is only their treatment that differs; unlike these landscapes," he waved his hand over them dismissively, "which appear to have been painted by an artist quite out of touch with recent styles."

Wen felt a growing unease. He cared little what the eunuch thought of his work but he began to worry about what the Emperor's reaction might be to his paintings. *What if the Emperor agrees with the eunuch? What if this entire journey was for nothing?* In the ensuing silence, Ming shot to his feet, hurried out the door onto the porch and vomited again into the flowers.

Several evenings later, Wen and Ming were invited by the eunuch to dine with him at a restaurant in the heart of the city. Yang Su, having other affairs to attend to, was unable to accompany them. Wen felt on edge, suspecting that Po Cheng planned something other than a pleasant meal.

While waiting for Po Cheng to arrive, Yang Su mentioned the eunuch's phenomenal rise in the Court. "He is now one of the wealthiest men in the capital which is astounding considering that a few short years ago he was a lowly palace-warden."

"A palace-warden?" Ming asked. "What is that?"

"The eunuch whose task it is to monitor the Emperor's concubines, ensuring their sexual loyalty. This is done by marking their bodies with a paste that comes from geckos fed on cinnabar that turns the lizards red. The lizards are then killed and pounded in mortars. It is believed the marks from the gecko paste will disappear if the concubine has illegitimate sexual intercourse. In this way, the Emperor can ensure no outsider is pleasuring himself in his harem."

"Does it actually work?" asked Ming.

"I have no idea. It is court tradition; that is enough."

Moments later, Po Cheng arrived in an enclosed palanquin on poles carried by eight sweating porters. Wen and Ming joined Po Cheng and the porters took them down into the bustling city. The eunuch was accompanied by a slim, frightened-looking boy, perhaps ten, who sat close to Po Cheng the entire trip and did not speak a word. Wen wondered if the boy was destined to be a eunuch too when the time came. In the meantime, he appeared to be Po Cheng's plaything.

Throughout the trip, a voluble Po chattered about his own importance at the Court, boasting about the high-placed people he knew, his closeness to the Emperor and the affairs of state. After railing against the power of the Buddhist hierarchy in the city, he praised his long relationship with Yang Su and how he valued his friendship.

"Since you arrived in Linan, have you met any people from the far north of our country?" Po Cheng asked Wen, not waiting for an answer. "Apparently, because of the great famines in the north in recent years, many people of those regions have come to Linan. The restaurant we are going to is owned by a northerner. I think you will find it of interest, especially Ming." In his excitement, he gave the little boy a squeeze, pulling him in tight and kissing the top of his head.

The heart of the city was a teeming cauldron of chaos. The crowds, seeking relief from the heat, had poured into the streets and alleys. Blocked by the congestion, the palanquin could go no further down the narrow lanes. They were forced to take to their feet and walk the last dozen blocks, shoving their way through a teeming crowd of revellers. They passed storytellers and street entertainers singing or declaiming ancient poems under red smoking lanterns that swung above the storefronts and restaurants. The air carried the pleasant scents of cooking food and smoke, and gamier smells of human effluents and rotting meat.

From low balconies, prostitutes with painted eyebrows purled fetchingly to possible customers and leaned out like willow catkins along a stream. In front of a tavern, a pair of singing girls adeptly juggled balls. No woman of good breeding would be seen in the entertainment district.

To Wen the crowds around him seemed in a frenzy of desperate celebration, as if they sensed the arrival of an all-engulfing darkness, the final approach of the Mongol hordes. Early that morning, instead of announcing the weather as usual, the Buddhist monks had sent up a hue and cry throughout the neighbourhood. "The Mongols are coming! Mongol horsemen are coming!" Mongol riders had been sighted at dawn on the road coming into Linan. Residents by the thousands had streamed down to the western gates, Wen and Ming among them, to meet thousands of others coming into the city seeking the protection of its walls and ramparts. Next to the Temple to the God of Walls and Moats, soldiers had swung the gates shut, beating people back with the flat sides of their swords, leaving crowds of desperate farmers and workers outside.

Soon, guards had announced from the ramparts that the riders were in fact several dozen of the Emperor's own soldiers on stolen Mongol horses, wearing Mongol clothing from captured prisoners. Although the crowds dispersed and returned home, Wen learned from his host that the soldiers had brought bad news – the city under siege, Xiangyang, was about to capitulate.

Wen began to feel uneasy. *Where is he taking us?* he wondered as Po Cheng walked ahead, his hand on the little boy's shoulder.

A man stopped Po and asked something, pointing at the child. Po shook his head. The man, looking disappointed, left, and they continued on.

Po stopped at a street-side seller of medicinal herbs and inspected the products laid out on a cloth. Wen asked the turbaned peddler what he was offering in his many ceramic bowls. The bug-eyed little man pointed at each concoction while repeating his sales chant: "Powdered rhinoceros horn for man's delight; crushed pearls for the same; snakeskin to place in the ears of the sick; spiders and earthworms for serious illness; a fly from the back of a dog – legs and wings removed – to cure the sickness that comes from evil air; centipedes boiled and powdered; a worm from high mountain streams to cure fever; powdered gold and mercury for long life; and a secret powder that ensures immortality."

Po bought a sachet of the last powder at a price Wen found unconscionable, as the handful of coins could buy enough rice to feed a family for half a year.

The little party moved on through the crowd. Three acrobats scuttled past walking on their hands with their heads between their legs, tiny monkeys leaping up and down on their backs. The crowd tossed nuts to the monkeys and coins to the acrobats. Po and the others then halted to watch an entertainer with a large tub of water in which swam several trained carp. As the entertainer called each fish by name, it would surface at one end of the tub and skittle across the top of the water balancing on its tail. While they stood watching, a young prostitute approached Ming. The pendants at her sash chimed and swayed suggestively. Smelling of the most intoxicating perfume – both sweet and earthy – she tried to entice him into a darkened doorway nearby. Glancing at her with alarm, Ming resisted until the young woman noticed a pair of passing soldiers and turned her attention to them, with more success.

A moment later, Po's entourage came upon a street artist who could cry with one half of his face and laugh with the other half, even as he brushed calligraphies of sad and happy poems simultaneously with both hands.

At the next corner, the party happened upon a soothsayer using the "narrow-neck" game to divine the future. Po showed the man a string of copper coins and motioned to Wen.

"The diviner will tell your fortune. I will pay. It is my gift to you," Po announced.

I don't want my fortune told, Wen thought. But he could not refuse as the man was moving into action and, no doubt, already counting on his payment.

At first Wen didn't know what to make of the man with long fingers squared-off at the tips. He watched in fascination while the fortune-teller tossed eight darts, one by one, bouncing them off a skin drum and into a narrow-necked pottery jug sitting on the ground. When done, he turned the jug upside down, dumping the contents in one swift motion onto a square white cloth. Kneeling before the cloth, he bent over, placing his face close to the darts. Suddenly opening his eyes wide, he stared at the lines before him. From the pattern of the darts, he pictured a written character, which would suggest the divination.

He turned to Wen. "The prophecy is for you?"

Wen nodded.

"The character I read is 'weixian.'" He pointed at the jumble of darts as he stood.

"Pah!" Po shouted. "The character is 'danger', you say? Tell us more – is it danger from a knife, an axe, a sword, a wild animal, a woman? Or perhaps it is danger from the Mongols?"

The soothsayer shrugged. "I know not."

"Danger from above or below? Danger today, tomorrow or after the next full moon?"

"I tell you I do not know."

"In the night? In full daylight?" Po persisted.

"I see one character. 'Danger.' That is all."

"Pah." Po threw the string of coins at the man's feet so he had to go down on his knees to gather them up.

Turning down the darkest alley in the quarter, they arrived at their destination, a restaurant which displayed no banner out front and no sign on the door. The small room was crowded, but, as their group entered, the owner, recognizing the important eunuch from the Court, shouted at four patrons to leave their table at the back and offered chairs to the new arrivals. The original diners seated themselves on the floor along the wall.

"What do you have tonight?" Po Cheng asked.

"All dishes from the north. Special dishes. You will like them."

A straggly beard hanging from his chin, the owner stood beside their table holding a board on which he had scratched the characters describing that day's specialties. At the top it read "two-legged mutton".

"What is this?" Wen asked.

"Food from the north," the owner replied, shrugging. "We had many famines in my home country. No food at all. We grew accustomed to eating anything."

Wen read down the list of specialties for the benefit of Ming: "There are four dishes offered. 'Young Girl', 'Child', 'Woman', 'Old Man'. I do not know what these dishes mean," he said to the owner.

"They mean exactly what they say. Do not worry – they are not our own people but enemies who have been captured and executed."

Ming's face went pale.

Wen turned and said, "You mean this is human flesh? You serve human flesh?"

"Of course. We grew to enjoy it in the north during those famine years. The meat is far superior to the best mutton or pork."

"I have heard of this happening among soldiers and peasants in dire circumstances but never in the midst of plenty. It disgusts me." Wen stood up from the table and Ming followed. "You have had your little joke, Po Cheng. We will find our way back on our own."

Po Cheng threw his head back and cackled while stroking the neck of the boy seated next to him. "You really should try it."

Wen and Ming left.

Heading back to the Hall of Pure Emptiness, Ming asked, "Why would the eunuch do such a thing?"

Wen shook his head. "The eunuch rather enjoys belittling us, Ming. He is an exceedingly strange man. In some ways, I actually feel sorry for him."

"Was it really human flesh they were serving?"

"I am afraid it was, yes."

～

For a month, Wen and Ming remained as guests of Yang Su and his wife. Over that time, Lady Yang grew fond of both visitors, spending many pleasant hours sitting with her guests in the gardens among the peonies, mimosas and orchids. She was a woman of refinement, no longer willow-waisted like the young beauties of the city, but one whose beauty had matured into elegance and dignity. Her clothing – the long skirt and jacket of dove grey silk, the purple scarf around her shoulders – announced that she was a woman of a wealthy and important family.

Lady Yang felt a particular friendship with Wen, based on their mutual love of the poetry of earlier dynasties. She could quote Li Po's works from memory and with genuine feeling. Sometimes she read aloud true-to-life ghost stories for her two guests from Hong Mai's popular collection, *Record of the Listener,* as she sat on a bench before a wall of chrysanthemums white as powdered flesh. She and Wen were intellectual equals, comfortable in each other's presence. The harmony of their temperaments had been apparent from the first moment they met and grew only deeper and stronger. At times, Yang Su would join their conversations in the garden and fill them in on the latest news and rumours circulating through the Court.

Lady Yang questioned Wen and Ming about their travels, encouraging Wen to talk about his paintings and life in the south. She was interested to hear what Ming too had to say about their long journey and encouraged him to speak about his labours with the peasants he had met along the way.

"It must be gruelling work for the farmers, bending over all day in the rice paddies," she observed. Her hair was coiled and held in place by ivory combs in the shape of phoenixes and flowers.

"Yes," Ming agreed. "It is the most difficult work I have ever done."

Late one morning, Lady Yang asked Wen: "Have you seen our orchid garden?"

When she learned that Wen had not yet stumbled upon it in his explorations about the grounds, she insisted they visit it immediately.

They took a winding path that led to the far side of the property. Here numerous varieties of orchids were in bloom in a shady grotto spotted with sunlight. Lady Yang pointed them out, giving their names. A tumble of white orchids foamed down a wall; a cluster of purple blossoms was visible next to a foursome of speckled black on yellow petals; one orchid with a red slit tongue was followed by another, scarlet and wet and slick as waxy exotic seaweed; another of three petals was so pure white, achingly white, it seemed as if it could live for a moment only; one orchid was speckled purple and white with two petal-wings and a white bulb of a head that resembled something alive, a lush butterfly, or a gorgeous moth that arises from the heart of a dying sage; and a final orchid was striped like a tiger's hide floating under water.

Wen watched Lady Yang as she gazed at the flowers. *In another life...we could have... In some ways she reminds me of the farm woman, the same dignity.*

She interrupted his reverie by turning to him and asking, "I've been wondering, Wen, what is your style name?"

"Ink Mountain."

～

Later that afternoon, Yang Su entered the garden from the house and approached as Wen and Lady Yang were discussing Po Cheng's paintings of orchids.

As he drew near, Lady Yang was saying, "I hope I do not shock you, Wen, but I confess to disliking his painting intensely. There is something false and sentimental about his work. I do not believe he is a true artist. You know, he is a man of prodigious wealth. How is it, I wonder, that a eunuch can assemble such a fortune? He goes about the court constantly whispering his intrigues, playing one faction against the other. He has the ear of the Emperor, is always at his side." Leaning closer to Wen, she lowered her voice. "And yet I have heard from my contacts in the harem that he is plotting to replace our present Emperor, to take the throne himself. These are rumours only, of course, but one never knows."

Yang Su, who did not hear the details of their conversation, nodded in greeting. "I have just received word. The invitation to the Court has come at last. You will present your paintings and deliver your message to the Emperor early tomorrow morning."

The next day they rose with the first light. Yang Su donned his most luxurious pale yellow robes and provided robes for Wen and Ming – for the former, a fine ceremonial outfit of deep royal blue trimmed in gold at the collar and sleeves, and for Ming, a simple but elegant robe of maroon trimmed in yellow.

As they gathered at the gate, Yang Su politely greeted them with crossed hands. "Good. We are ready. The palanquin will drop us at the entrance to the Imperial grounds and we will walk from there. It is not far."

In his left hand, Wen held the bamboo tube with the long-life paintings. He held his other hand lightly over his heart, for within his robes he had placed the simple bamboo brush that hid the message from One Tooth for the Emperor.

The palanquin brought them to the well-guarded Gate of the Eastern Flowering. Entering the vast grounds of the palace, they walked along the Imperial Way. The promenade was lined with low stone walls beyond which were the private imperial grounds of sculpted mounds and planted forests known as Phoenix Hill. Wen stopped and pointed over the wall. "What is that? What are they doing?" In the distance, halfway up a rise topped by a cluster of ornamental trees, a dozen court servants held two trussed deer on the ground. While four or five of the servants kneeled on each deer to keep the kicking and thrashing of the frightened animals from injuring anyone, several other servants were gathered about the deers' heads.

Yang Su explained. "It is believed that the deer know how to find a secret grass which they eat, a grass that is said to keep death at bay. The servants are collecting scrapings from the tongues of the deer. The Emperor will eat these in another attempt to ensure his immortality."

Eventually, they came to a towering gate topped by sinuous dragon sculptures of gold-painted wood and guarded by eight soldiers in light shining armour. Beyond the gate lay the entrance to the Mountain of Heaven Hall where the Emperor would receive them. Yang Su explained their business to the captain of the guard and the trio was led through the gate and into a side room, which contained a capacious stone bath. Here, they bathed quickly and were then doused with fragrant powders by a servant. After re-donning their ceremonial robes, they were each given a pellet of herbs to chew, tasting of anise and clove, so their breath would not offend or contaminate the Emperor. The soldiers then led them into the hall.

The long ceremonial room stretched before them, its high ceiling supported by gold-painted columns, its walls decorated with swirling depictions of birds, beasts and flowers. At the far end, seven wide steps led to the raised throne mounted on stone lions where the Emperor already sat, adorned in brocade robes of brilliant purple. The dragon embroidered on the front of his robes seemed to writhe with the Emperor's every move, twitching and flashing among its stitched clouds of shimmering silk. On his head, the Emperor wore a ritual black silk headpiece, short black rods protruding from the sides.

On the top step, just below the Son of Heaven, stood three of the ministers of the council. The remainder of the staircase held members of the Court, the chancellery and the imperial secretariat. The floor of the hall was filled with retainers, scholars, academicians, imperial guards and a dozen of the most esteemed court painters.

Standing to the left of the Son of Heaven, dressed in silk robes of forest green, stood Po Cheng, Director of the Painting Academy, and First Minister Jia Sidao, in crimson robes, his eyes constantly scanning the crowd.

To the Emperor's right, juniper smoke drifted up from an immense incense burner that was twice the size of the throne and resembled a range of mountains.

On entering the hall, Ming threw himself to the floor in prostration, knocking his head on the flagstones out of respect and fear. He was helped up by a soldier who bid him accompany Wen and Yang Su to a place at the foot of the stairs before the Emperor's throne where all three kowtowed.

When the three guests had risen from their low bows, the Captain of the Guard cried out, "Ten-thousand years! Long live His Celestial Magnificence!" and all present replied with shouts, "Ten-thousand years! Ten-thousand years to *Huangdi*!"

As Emperor Duzong leaned aside and whispered to the eunuch, Wen studied him: the Emperor's long smooth face lacked a moustache or beard; the mouth was thin and tight and he continually licked his lips. His half-closed eyes were black and sharp as shiny beetles. Again the Emperor leaned toward Po Cheng who listened a moment. The eunuch nodded, then announced, "Li Wen, painter from the south, step forward and speak."

Wen, grasping the large bamboo tube, took a step, kowtowed

again and stood. "Your Majesty, Most Excellent Son of Heaven, I bear long-life gifts from your esteemed servant, my master, Fu Wei. Four paintings, as well as a message for Your Excellency."

At the mention of a message, the eunuch, while attempting to hide his interest, stared more intently at Wen.

The Emperor leaned forward. He spoke slowly. "I remember Fu Wei well. He was my childhood tutor and always treated me kindly." His voice was surprisingly high and world-weary. "In my loneliness, without other children with whom to play, he became a child for me, although he was a scholar of great learning and ability. You bear a message from him, after all this time? And four paintings? Are they the work of Fu Wei himself?"

"No, Your Excellency. I, your humble servant, Li Wen, a simple and unskilled artist, was instructed by Fu Wei, my teaching master, to paint these landscapes of the four seasons on my journey here from our city in the south. They are a long-life gift for Your Excellency from my teacher."

"Come. Let us view these paintings."

Wen was directed to mount the stairs. Standing before the throne, he began sliding the paintings from the tube. Imperial servants appeared in order to hold them up for Duzong's viewing. Soon all four paintings were displayed in a semi-circle before the Emperor, who turned his head from side to side, contemplating the works. Wen remained standing, head bowed before the Son of Heaven who appeared to be captivated by the landscapes before him.

When the Emperor's eyes rested on the painting of winter, in its snowy brilliance, a profound and mysterious silence settled for a few moments on the hall.

When the Emperor turned his gaze to the spring painting with the monastery in the distance, an iron bell tolled subtly on the air, a distant sound that seemed to come from deep within the landscape. In that moment, a tiny golden bird flitted down from the rafters of the hall, tried to land on a pine bough and disappeared, vanishing into the forest in the painting.

Next, the Emperor considered the painting of autumn, and a rumble of distant thunder rolled through the hall. He looked up a moment, wondering.

His eyes then fell on the painting of summer and the Emperor smiled, for he understood that the great lone mountain depicted there was meant to represent him, the Emperor of all China, the Son of Heaven rising up at the centre of his universe.

From the corner of his eye, Wen could see the subtle sneer on Po Cheng's face, while the Emperor continued to give the paintings his deepest attention.

The Emperor turned to Li Wen and said, "Fu Wei has offered the Son of Heaven a marvellous gift. These are indeed harmonious landscapes. Nothing I have seen can compare with them. Tell me, eunuch," he turned toward Po Cheng, "what do you think of them?"

"Your Majesty, the works are indeed harmonious and well-executed, but I believe they are painted in a rather archaic style."

Ignoring the eunuch's comment, Emperor Duzong turned his attention back to Li Wen. "You also mentioned a message for me from your master, yes?"

"Indeed, Your Majesty." Wen reached into his robes and removed the small length of bamboo brush that held the message from One Tooth. Going down on one knee and holding out his arms with the bamboo brush resting across his open palms, he bowed his head and offered the message to the Son of Heaven.

"A brush?"

"The message is hidden inside the handle, Your Majesty."

Taking the small bamboo tube, Emperor Duzong extracted the single sheet of rice paper, thoughtlessly handing the now-empty brush to Po Cheng. The Emperor's face was impassive as he read the message from Fu Wei.

Wen tried not to let any emotion show. He stared at the floor, waiting.

A tense silence hung on the air. Wen glanced up. Still the Emperor's face remained blank, indecipherable. He finished reading the message and leaned to his right, the sheet in his hand. Stretching his arm out to its full length, the Emperor touched the paper to the glowing coals within the incense burner next to his throne.

In a moment, the message was in flames.

∾

"What will happen to the paintings now?" Ming asked Yang Su on their return to the Hall of Pure Emptiness following the audience with the Emperor. Wen listened closely to the response.

"First they will be entered into the Imperial painting catalogue. After that, it will be up to the Emperor. He may have them displayed in one of his private chambers for a while. Sometimes he has his favourite paintings moved to the hall where he meets with his ministers so he can view them while making decisions of state. Or perhaps he will enjoy them in the imperial residence with his concubines. It is hard to say. Why do you ask?"

"I have come to love these works," Ming tried to explain to Yang Su. "They are more than just paintings of landscape – they represent a year of Wen's life and the heart of our friendship. It was the paintings that convinced me to come on this journey with him at the start. I thought a man who could paint like that could teach me much about how to look at the world."

The next day, they received an invitation from Po Cheng to be his guests at a shadow puppet play at a theatre in an old part of the city. After the experience at the 'two-legged mutton' restaurant, Wen and Ming had been hesitant to accept yet another invitation from the eunuch but Yang Su had encouraged them to attend with him: "I am sure you will enjoy it. Po Cheng is an important official in the Society of Painted Leather, the friends of shadow theatre. The eunuch himself is the patron of the troupe we will see, which usually presents traditional myths. But tonight he himself has written a special play for the occasion. You must come."

That evening, Yang Su, Wen and Ming arrived at the Purple

Bamboo Theatre in an enclosed palanquin carried by eight bearers. Entering the theatre crowded with well-off patrons talking excitedly, they took their seats on a bench in the front row and waited for the play to begin. Next to Ming was seated a scholar and his wife.

"Have you seen the players before?" asked Ming.

"Yes, many times. They are an excellent troupe. I am sure you will enjoy them," the scholar said and smiled.

The eunuch himself was nowhere to be seen.

Sounds drifted in from backstage, two stringed instruments, the tapping of a drum and the occasional bleat of a horn. A transparent white cloth screen had been stretched across the width of the stage. Behind this sheet, lanterns were lit. Once the show started, the puppeteers would hold the puppets close to the screen, the bright light from the lanterns behind projecting the puppets' shadows onto the sheet without revealing the puppeteers, who remained invisible while they operated the puppets using rods and strings.

The five-man troupe filed out from backstage and stood in front of the screen, bowing and introducing themselves. Their leader noted that they were about to present "a most humble show, certainly not excellent enough for tonight's august audience."

Yang Su leaned over to his two guests and whispered, "They are considered by far the best troupe in the capital. The master, on the far left, is known as Two-Hands Chang – he can simultaneously operate the strings for two puppets, one with each hand."

"We wish all of our guests long life and prosperity, and that you enjoy our simple play," the master said to the audience. With that, the troupe filed out, disappearing backstage.

A moment later, the shadows of two puppets appeared on the illuminated sheet. Through the sheer screen the audience could discern the finest movements of the puppets, which had jointed limbs and could move and dance and jump like living beings.

The taller of the two figures pauses, bows, adjusts the sleeves of his robe and runs his hand over his bald head, indicating he is a Buddhist monk. *The second figure, clearly a monkey, bows more deeply, his head banging on the floor, and promptly jumps up and down. The two characters approach a third figure, an old man sitting by the gate to the city, weeping.*

Monk: "Greetings, venerable father. My monkey and I have come over the mountains from the distant South to see the Emperor, the Son of Heaven, on his throne here in the capital. Why do you weep?"

Old man: "Greetings, honourable monk and little monkey from the South. I weep because year after year, I prepare the fifty learned essays in advance and I take the official examinations to become a scholar, and year after year, I fail them. And now, my old wife, who I honour greatly, says she is sorely disappointed in me. She says she will turn back into a white snake demon and disappear if I fail the exam once again. She says she was a white snake demon before she ever met me. I never suspected."

Monk: "When is the exam?"

Old man: "Tomorrow."

Monk: "Don't weep, old one. With the aid of the excellent Guanyin, goddess of compassion, we will help you."

The monkey holds a porcelain bowl under the old man's eyes.

Old man: "What are you doing, little monkey?"

Monkey: "Collecting your tears, honourable elder. With these, we will ensure your wife remains human, for anyone who drinks human tears cannot long remain a white snake demon. We will sneak the tears into her cup of tea."

Monk: "Come with us, old man. Let us go to see your wife."

With the first words of the play, Wen tensed, realizing that the eunuch was mocking them. Ming, for his part, appeared to be riveted by the entertainment and was oblivious to any ridicule.

The trio walks beside West Lake.

Monk: "Tell me, honourable father, how you happened to marry a white snake demon?"

Old man: "It was many years ago, when I was young. I was enjoying a walk on a spring day, right here beside West Lake. A poem written two hundred years ago by Ou Yang Hsiu was wafting through my memory, like windblown blossoms from plum trees, 'The lovely Spring breeze has come / Back to the Lake of the West'."

The monkey tumbles along beside the other two, doing somersaults and back flips.

Old man continues: "Suddenly dark clouds flew from over the mountains and massed together in the sky. It felt as if night was coming on. The birds fell silent. Then, a flash of lightning!"

As the stage area grows darker, lightning is seen and thunder heard.

Old man: "Luckily, I had brought a parasol which I raised over my head against the driving rain. I noticed a young woman nearby getting soaked. Her willow-like waist was so narrow I believed that I could encircle it with my two hands, and her feet were no larger than persimmons. She wore her hair in the traditional 'falling-from-your-horse chignon', and she had red dots painted on her dimples. This most exquisite maiden was thoroughly soaked through with the rain. Our eyes met and I naturally invited her to share my umbrella."

To the sound of rain falling, the monkey, still carrying the pot of tears, prances about with an umbrella.

Old man: "Under that umbrella, we walked three times around West Lake. Her voice was like the breeze that sighs through the first budding leaves. The rain released the aromatic powders of spring on the air. Her skin smelled of aloes and sandalwood. I was bewitched."

Monk: "Old man, I am a monk. I know nothing of love but may I ask you a question?"

Old man: "Of course, honourable young monk."

Monk: "Do you love this woman still, now that you know she was once a white snake demon?"

Old man: "White snake, black snake, green or blue, I would love her still. Not that she is always easy to get along with. She tries me in a thousand different ways – but I love her anyway."

Monkey: "Will there be tea when we reach your house?"

Old man: "Yes, little monkey, there will be Mountain Goddess Tea to drink."

In the next scene, the trio arrives at the house of the old man. The old woman is there, making tea.

Old man: "How did you know we wanted tea?"

Old woman: "You always want tea. You were due to return so I made tea."

Monkey: "Is it Mountain Goddess Tea?"

Old woman: "Yes, it is. But you are a little monkey, how is it you are able to speak?"

The monkey shrugs his shoulders and does a back flip.

Two soldiers arrive.

First soldier: "Are you Monk Wang from the South?"

Monk: "Yes."

First soldier: "We have word that you are a painter and have brought a landscape painting as a long-life gift for the Emperor."

Monk: "This is true, good soldiers. But how is it you know this?"

Second soldier: "We have reports that the monkey was seen painting the landscape instead of you. To have a monkey do a painting for the Emperor is a serious ridicule of the Son of Heaven."

The monkey runs to and fro waving a paintbrush in the air.

Monk: "This is not true. The monkey simply loves to play with my brushes. He does not paint."

First soldier: "He was seen doing the painting. You are under arrest."

Old woman: "The tea is ready. Soldiers of the most august Emperor, will you join us?"

Both soldiers: "Yes, we will, good mother, because the execution grounds are dusty at this time of year. And when we have finished our tea, we will lead the monk and the monkey to their fate."

The monkey does a back flip and empties the bowl of tears into the old woman's cup while she is distracted pouring tea for the soldiers and the others. Everyone drinks.

Old man: "This is terrible, honourable monk. I will weep bitter tears if you and little monkey are executed. And now you will not be able to intercede with the goddess, Guanyin, for me. I will never pass the exam."

Monk: "Do not worry, venerable old one. I will intercede with the goddess for you. She will have mercy and let you pass the exam. I am sure of it."

Old man: "If I pass the exam, esteemed monk, I will go to the temple and bow before the column of K'uei, God of Literature, and fill the air with the smoke of incense to express my gratitude to Heaven."

Old woman: "Old husband, listen to me. Do not worry. I will stay with you, even if you fail the exam again. I will not return to being a white snake demon. I am too old for all that. Besides, now we must do what we can to help save our guests, this honourable monk and his silly monkey."

First soldier: "We have finished our tea. Let us go now to the execution grounds."

Monk: "Come, little monkey, good friend. Let us go to meet our fate."

In the next scene, the two soldiers, the monk and his monkey arrive at the execution grounds, recognizable by three skulls mounted on posts.

Monkey, pointing at the three skulls, claps his hands, and jumps up and down: "Look, good Monk Wang, three skulls in a row!"

Monk: "Perhaps it is a sign that the White Tiger of the West will come to save us."

First soldier: "Prepare the place of execution!"

Second soldier: "Yes, sir!"

Monkey, standing at attention (in a high-pitched, mocking voice): "Prepare the place of execution!"

The hooded figure of the Executioner enters, carrying an axe in one hand and a long knife in the other.

First soldier: "Greetings, esteemed Imperial Executioner. I hope you are well. Do you have your orders?"

Executioner: "Yes. First we flay the monkey; then we behead the monk. Then we burn their bodies."

The monkey starts running around in circles, as smoke appears behind the stage.

First soldier: "Grab that monkey!"

The second soldier grabs the monkey and holds him. The Executioner approaches, his long knife raised.

Monk: "Wait, kind Executioner. Do you smell smoke?"

A bellow comes from the rear of the stage: "Fire! Fire!"

The Executioner stops and stares at smoke billowing out from behind the screen: "Look, good soldiers of the Emperor, the city is on fire! We must flee to West Lake!"

First soldier: "Yes, honourable Executioner. You are right. We must help fight the fire. The executions can wait."

The audience shifted uneasily. The entire theatre was quickly filling with smoke. In an attempt to create sufficient smoke for the play, the troupe had ignited a large pot of half-dry leaves backstage. But the leaves had burned higher and more quickly than expected and one fiery leaf had floated up and away and landed on the stage screen, setting the fine cloth afire. Soon the entire stage area was burning. Yang Su glanced about, "Run, my friends! This is not part of the play!" Already the audience was fleeing into the street, shouting 'Fire! Fire!'

Although the theatre was partially burned and the play could not be continued, a lack of wind that evening made it possible to contain and quickly extinguish the flames before it spread to neighbouring buildings. But Wen considered it one more omen in a series of inauspicious signs.

∼

Wen rested on a comfortable stone bench in the garden, leaning back against a gingko tree, contemplating a wall of blazing white chrysanthemums. The breezeless afternoon was laden with humidity. Wen stared at the flowers and drifted into sleep. One moment he was there, the next he was swallowed into white.

A few minutes later, Ming approached Wen to announce that the eunuch had come calling. The sleeping Wen looked at peace and Ming decided not to wake him.

Ming returned to the house and told Po Cheng, "The master and Lady Yang are out, accompanied by their servants, and Li Wen is asleep in the garden."

The eunuch nodded. "It matters not. It is you with whom I wish to speak."

Ming was apprehensive as he led Po Cheng to the music pavilion where they sat.

"I trust you enjoyed the play, Ming? My deepest apologies that it was cut short by the fire."

"I have never seen such skilled artists."

"Yes, we will definitely have you again, as soon as we find another theatre. Now, to the reason for my visit. I have a question," the eunuch began.

Later, when Wen awoke from his slumber, Ming was sitting on the ground next to him, waiting. "Ah, Ming," Wen said, "I fell asleep."

"The eunuch called while you slept."

"You should have awakened me. What did he want?"

"He came to ask how we enjoyed the play. Then he asked me to tell him of our travels."

"And, did you?"

"I did, yes; but I fear that I may have said too much. I believe I became carried away in the telling. The eunuch usually frightens me, but today he was different – friendly."

"What happened?"

"He said that the night of our great feast, I had mentioned something about a tomb. To tell the truth, I had taken too much drink to be able to remember anything I said that night. And today, once I started talking I lost control of my tongue. I fell into boasting of our finding the tomb's treasures. His interest in my story increased considerably on hearing of it. Did I err?"

"Yes, Ming, you did. I thought we agreed that the tomb was never to be mentioned to anyone. Po Cheng is the sort of man who would love nothing more than to add to his riches by desecrating a tomb."

Ming bowed his head low. "When he asked if the tomb could be located in one of your paintings, I told him where to find it."

"I suspect you wanted to enrich your story with wonders that would impress the eunuch and make him think well of you, yes?"

"It is true. I am deeply shamed."

"What's done is done. In any case, it is highly unlikely that the eunuch or anyone else could find the tomb's location simply based on my painting."

"Still, I feel I am no more than an ignorant peasant, just as the eunuch says." Ming stared at his thick hands folded in his lap and said no more. His heart began to race with the sudden realization that he had also revealed the name of the mountain in the painting of spring. The eunuch would have little trouble locating Mount Tung.

The next day, Po Cheng prepared to document and register the four paintings presented to the Emperor by Li Wen. Sitting in his office in the Painting Academy, dark shelves on the walls filled with ancient catalogues, he folded open the official Imperial Catalogue of Paintings on the table before him. The catalogue consisted of large loose leaves bound into an album that listed in detail the innumerable artworks given to the Emperor during his reign.

As the eunuch ground the ink, he wondered about the message to the Emperor and what it might have contained. *And why did the Emperor burn it?*

Also, the discussion with the peasant, Ming, the day before had confirmed his suspicions, first raised at Yang Su's feast for the visitors. *These two fools from the south did indeed stumble across a tomb during their travels, a tomb that surely contained objects of inestimable value.* The eunuch had no doubt he could locate the tomb, Wen's painting of spring serving as a veritable map.

The paintings hung before him. He inspected them closely to determine the exact route taken by the two travellers. His knowledge of that part of the world – he himself was from the north – was insufficient to determine with any accuracy the location of the tomb, but he had no doubt that he could find it with the help of colleagues from the region who would certainly know the location of Mount Tung.

Po Cheng began to make his entries in the catalogue. He dipped his brush and wrote the characters down the page: *Four landscape paintings, one of each of the four seasons, executed by a little-known amateur artist of the southern provinces, Li Wen. * A long-life gift from Fu Wei, former tutor to the Son of Heaven, Emperor Duzong. Long ago, Scholar Fu was sent into exile in the south. * Little is known about precise locations depicted in the four paintings, except that they are regions to the south and west of the capital. * Delivered to the Court of Emperor Duzong by the painter Li Wen himself, in the seventh lunar month of the ninth year of the reign.*

Late that day, the scorching sun melted into West Lake outside the Painting Academy. Rolling up the four paintings, the eunuch made his way to a scheduled meeting with the Emperor.

Seated on a small throne in his antechambe, Emperor Duzong eyed the eunuch. "You have not asked me what was in the message from my former tutor. Why?"

"Your Excellency, it would be impertinent of me to ask. I am sure you burned it for a good reason."

"As the Emperor, I do not need a good reason. I do as I wish, when I wish. Do not forget that, eunuch. Nevertheless, I will tell you what the message contained because I believe you should hear it. Fu Wei claims that this painter from the south, Li Wen, is the greatest painter he has ever seen and should be appointed Director of the Imperial Academy of Painting immediately. He would replace you, of course."

Po Cheng was silent. He turned and gazed out the window, noticed how fast the low scattered clouds were scudding across the sky.

In that silence, the Emperor came to a decision not to reveal to the eunuch the next line of the message which he recalled precisely: *Whosoever tells Your Excellency that these paintings are not the greatest in the Middle Kingdom is a liar, a traitor and a threat to the Imperial Court.* Duzong thought, *A message carried over distant mountains and delivered directly to the Emperor is like a message from the gods and cannot be ignored.*

"What is your response, eunuch? Is he a great painter or not?"

"There is no doubt he exhibits a certain skill, Your Excellency, a rare talent even, but I believe he poses a great danger. Danger for you, danger for your Court."

"What do you mean?"

"Your Majesty, one could be both a great painter and still a traitor. It has been seen before. Do not be duped by the skill of this artist. I have studied the paintings closely and have discovered their subtle and dangerous intent. I respectfully suggest that you view them in this light, as I believe they were intended. Though meant as a long-life gift to Your Excellency, I have found that the paintings by Li Wen are filled with images of dissent and treachery. As you know, there exists a tradition among rebellious artists and scholars throughout the realm to use their paintings and poems to disguise negative opinions of Your Most August Emperor, your Court and your reign."

"I recognize no dissent in these works."

"I agree that the artist is subtle, but be assured that they contain certain coded images common to landscapes that can be interpreted in many different ways. To take an example – this painting of spring depicts a stand of mottled bamboo. As you know, I am sure, tradition has it that the mottling of bamboo is caused by falling tears. Among the painters of dissent, falling tears is a code for their feeling of disappointment at not finding a great ruler."

The eunuch pointed again. "These fallen leaves mean that great men have been cast aside by the Court. And, the dark clouds, here, suggest the lack of a warming sun, that is, a cold-hearted Emperor who refuses to nurture the people, which is exactly how the dissenters have been referring to Your Majesty. I denounce in the strongest terms this Li Wen who proclaims disharmony in the realm through his landscapes. His works show great irreverence toward Your Majesty. They mark Li Wen as a traitor."

"This is not a charge that can be made lightly. It brings a penalty of death."

"Your Majesty, I am convinced of his treachery; but I do not stand alone in this judgment. Renowned painters of the Academy agree with my assessment and are willing to denounce the works as well as the artist."

The Emperor leaned forward to consider the landscape before him. "Look at the painting of summer. The towering mountain depicted there standing alone. It clearly reveals the high esteem in which Li Wen regards the Emperor. How can all you say be true in the light of this one image?"

"Your Majesty, the painter uses the great mountain as a form of false reverence, to draw your attention away from other details. Look closely. There is more. You see here? The mountain's base is lost in a banner of thick fog. The artist is stating quite clearly that the mountain stands on nothing, that the Emperor's rule stands on nothing. This is unconscionable."

The Emperor leaned forward again, looking closely and, for the first time, nodded. Po Cheng, excited at the prospect that he was succeeding at turning the Emperor's mind against Li Wen, still managed to maintain an air of humility. The eunuch indicated one painting after another, his voice rising, "Clouds and rain represent deceitful ministers; monkeys suggest slanderous speech in the Court; the rustling of the wind in the trees hints at a government in disarray. The evidence against the painter Li Wen is overwhelming and utterly damning."

The Emperor paused. His thoughts were confused. *Li Wen could indeed be both a great painter and a traitor. It is possible, as the eunuch says.* Emperor Duzong seethed. "I cannot allow anything that encourages dissent in the realms. Too many treacherous scholars and artists have begun to boldly express their criticisms of the Court and the Emperor. It cannot be allowed to continue. Having the Mongol enemies is quite enough – I don't need internal enemies as well."

"Your Majesty, I suggest you make an example of this Li Wen and his peasant companion." Emboldened by the success of his poisonous words, the eunuch bent to the Emperor's ear and whispered, "Shall I send soldiers to arrest them?"

In the middle of the night, Wen awoke and, before opening his eyes, noticed that the air smelled of a faint powdery perfume. He looked up to see Lady Yang leaning over him, holding a candle lantern, "Wen, I am sorry to disturb you, but please awake and listen to me."

Something in the urgency of her voice brought Wen shooting to the surface. Raising his head from the porcelain headrest, he forced his eyes to open wide. "Lady Yang? What is it? What is wrong?"

"Please dress quickly and follow me into the garden."

Moments later, to the scratching of crickets, they walked along one of the garden paths lit silver by the moon. Thick scents of mature summer, orchid and oleander, arose from the garden greenery around them.

She turned and grasped his forearm. "You and Ming must flee the city immediately. Do not wait for morning. Great danger awaits you here."

"Why? What has happened?"

"I have word from the harem – completely trustworthy information – that your lives are in danger."

"Why must we leave? I do not understand."

"The eunuch's poisonous words have turned the Emperor against you. Po Cheng's jealously knows no bounds. The Emperor confided to the eunuch the contents of the message from Fu Wei that you delivered."

Li Wen shook his head. "But the Emperor burned the message. I witnessed it myself."

"Despite burning it, Emperor Duzong apparently clearly recalled the contents of the message. He said that your teacher recommended that the Emperor appoint you immediately as Director of the Painting Academy, to replace the eunuch. Fu Wei said you are the greatest master of landscape he had seen in his lifetime, the greatest painter ever to have wielded a brush in the Middle Kingdom. He said that in your works inner and outer harmony mesh to perfection. Fu Wei claimed that if the Emperor were to recognize you in this way, by appointing you Director of the Academy, he would be praised for his wisdom and good judgment for ten thousand years."

Wen stared at the ground. "I am greatly honoured and greatly humbled by my master's words. I had no idea this was the message I carried for so long."

"There is more to tell. The eunuch knows how to insinuate himself into His Majesty's good graces. His words are poison but penetrating. Despite your master's praise, Po Cheng convinced the Emperor to have you and Ming arrested and executed as political dissenters."

"On what basis?"

"He claimed that your paintings are filled with coded images of rebellion, a common enough occurrence among scholars and artists who oppose the realm."

"What nonsense!"

"Without a doubt, the eunuch is devious and nurses unbounded jealousy. He also told His Majesty that even if the paintings are indeed great works of art, executing you will ensure that you will produce no further works for any other sovereign."

Their nighttime walk through the garden had brought them to the hidden corner where the orchids were in bloom. The moonlight set the flowers aglow. They halted and continued their conversation in low voices.

"How could this have happened?" he asked.

"Do not underestimate the devices of the eunuch."

"But this is untrue. There are no secret codes."

"Yes; but sadly, no censors or grand councillors in the Court today have the will to speak the truth to Emperor Duzong. They have seen how every criticism of the Emperor, however slight, is met with severe reprisals and charges of treason."

Wen nodded, bowed his head and sighed. "As the sovereign goes, so go the people and the kingdom. Confucius warned long ago that the deviations and errors of the Emperor would lead to the fall of the realm. Even the Emperor must be subservient to Confucian principles."

"I fear that my husband and I will be exiled in the inevitable purge, despite our unending loyalty to the sovereign. I feel it in the air – our world, I believe, is coming to an end." She shook her head as if to put such heavy thoughts from her mind. "You must leave without delay. We have spoken much too long as it is, but I could not bear to see you hurry off too quickly." Pulling her mauve silk wrap more tightly around her against the damp of night, she added. "It should not end like this, but I fear it must. Yang Su has been called to the Court to justify why he welcomed you and Ming as honoured guests, so he will be unable to say farewell. You must leave now before it is too late. Out of grief, I have kept you far too long."

At that moment, they both turned towards a commotion on the street near the entrance gate – the sound of shouts and heavy knocking caught their attention.

Suddenly Ming appeared beside Wen and Lady Yang. "What is it? What is happening? I hear soldiers."

"Go, now! Please hurry!" the Lady said. "By the back gate through the far garden." She pointed, a devastated look on her face. "From the city's western gate, you will see a monastery halfway up a mountain to the northwest. Go there. Mention my name to the abbot. They will take you in. Hurry!"

Wen and Ming ran off into the darkness.

Moments later, creeping out from the back gate, they glimpsed a company of soldiers carrying torches, bursting through the front entrance of the Hall of Pure Emptiness. Wen and Ming stuck to the shadows, hurrying down the Hill of Ten Thousand Pines into the narrow black alleys of the city where the light of the moon had never entered.

As they scuttled from doorway to doorway along the unlit sombre streets, Wen explained to Ming why they were forced to flee.

Ming moaned. "The eunuch's jealousy has destroyed us."

"No. Whatever eats at the heart of Po Cheng destroys only him."

"What will we do?"

"First, we must flee the city, but it will be impossible to exit the gates at night. We must wait for morning."

"Surely the Emperor's soldiers will be watching the gates?"

"No doubt. Perhaps we can slip out when the crowds of field labourers exit shortly after dawn. We will try to disguise ourselves in whatever way we can."

When they neared the western gate, they saw that it was shut for the night as they had expected. Several soldiers stood about with torches, questioning anyone who passed by. The two friends crept off into a nest of dusty alleys. Far down an empty lane, they slumped to the ground, leaned against a wall, and waited for morning. Wen tried to think of a disguise but with only the clothing on their backs, nothing came to mind. Finally, he fell into a fitful, anxious doze.

Several hours later, Wen and Ming were startled awake by the bleat of the gate-opening horns. When the first light of day unrolled high above the alley, they heard the drone of distant voices.

Wen glanced down the lane. "The gates are being opened. The field labourers are gathering."

"What will we do? If we are caught, they will execute us."

Wen hung his head. "I am truly sorry to have brought you into this danger, my friend." In looking down at his feet, Wen noticed the powdery pale grey dust of the alley. "I have an idea."

He cupped a handful of the fine powder and rubbed it into his hair, lightening it by several shades. Rubbing more dust in, he asked Ming, "Is it aging me? Does my hair turn grey before your eyes?"

"Yes, it works. Though it is not a perfect disguise, you certainly look far older now than before."

Wen picked up more handfuls of powder and rubbed it into Ming's hair. "We will be two old grandfathers heading off with the crowds to work in the fields."

After dusting themselves grey, Wen stood. "We must go, while the masses of labourers are at their thickest."

They edged out of the alley and eyed the gate in the distance. The three soldiers on guard were having difficulty inspecting every individual among the dense waves of morning workmen elbowing their way through the gate, which had just been opened for the gathered crowd. A torrent of humanity surged through, along with carts, palanquins and horses, a disordered, tumultuous throng in turmoil and confusion. Hundreds of men and animals were attempting to squeeze through the funnel of the city's main western gate. The crowd was fearful of the soldiers who were plucking random individuals from the chaos, questioning them and, when the simple workers responded with confused looks, slapping and beating them with sticks and the sides of their swords. The crowd continued flowing around the soldiers, like a stream curling around rocks in its flow.

"Follow me." Wen pushed his way into the mass of workers. Spotting a phalanx of farmers who were tall and broad, and who carried hoes on their shoulders, he and Ming edged forward, heads lowered, keeping these workers between them and the soldiers who, in any case, were busily occupied beating an uncomprehending peasant. Like a flood bursting through a break in an embankment, the throng surged through the gate, carrying Wen and Ming with them, out of the city and onto the tree-lined road beyond the walls.

After hurrying some distance down the road, they paused behind a thick willow tree by the waters of West Lake. "What are we to do now?" Ming asked. "Where will we go?"

Wen, shading his eyes with his hand, gazed up into the hills and beyond. "Lady Yang mentioned a monastery to the northwest." He pointed. "Do you see it there, in the distance, on the side of that mountain? We will go there, as she suggested. But first, let us wash the dust from our heads in the lake."

The two friends headed toward the mountain. After feeling wary for the first hour and checking the road behind constantly, Wen began to feel sure that they were not being followed. It seemed all his worries were falling away behind him. Walking along at an easy pace, Wen realized he was glad to be out of the city. The air was pure and clean. The sun, high in the heavens, filtered down through the golden leaves of a beech grove. Speckles of shadow danced along the ground with each breeze.

"It is good to be in the forest again."

Ming nodded. "The city was a wondrous place, full of excitement, entertainments, marvellous food – but, yes, it is good to be here."

"The city was filled also with unhappiness and discontent. It made my heart ache to see it."

"Yes. As you predicted the night before we entered."

They walked along the wide, well-used trail in silence.

Wen had a premonition that he and Ming would soon be parting. *I will miss you, my loyal friend. I will miss you.*

In late morning, they approached the monastery and Wen rapped on the old wooden gate rippled with cracks. A tall, sharp-eyed monk appeared.

"We bring greetings from Lady Yang to your abbot. We also seek a quiet hall in which to meditate, and a bowl of rice if possible."

Without hesitation, the monk stepped aside, let them in and closed the gate behind them.

Two days after arriving at the monastery, Wen and Ming were summoned by the tall monk to the stone-paved courtyard. Lady Yang awaited them on the far side. A languid breeze moved her emerald-green robes in such a way that, standing with her back to them, she resembled a morning glory bud still wrapped in its sheath. Next to her stood a scowling servant Wen recognized from the Yang household. Wen saw with great joy and relief that he was holding their packs with all their worldly goods, including his brushes, his ink sticks and so on.

After Wen thanked Lady Yang profusely, the old bent-over abbot of the monastery came out to greet Lady Yang. He then led them to a quiet room where they could talk and have tea.

As they sat at a lacquered table sipping from their cups, Lady Yang gazed outside in silence. Wen and Ming waited for her to speak. Finally, she turned to them. "In three days, Yang Su and I will head to exile in the south. The Emperor was displeased that his soldiers were not able to prevent your escape. As a result, my husband has fallen out of favour with the Court. There was some talk among the ministers that he be put to death, but the eunuch spoke on his behalf. Po Cheng pointed out that Yang Su has been a loyal servant to the sovereign for many years and the Emperor took this into consideration. His Majesty has decided to spare my husband's life, but ordered us into exile. How strange that my husband, in the end, owed his life to Po Cheng. I suppose the eunuch greatly valued his friendship, despite everything. The eunuch, poor man, did not have many friends."

"You speak of him as if he were gone."

"Yes. The struggle between First Minister Jia and the eunuch has come to an end. Jia has many friends in high places, including generals of the army, and they managed to turn the Emperor against Po Cheng, claiming that you escaped because the eunuch had warned my husband. I hear that the message you brought also had something to do with the eunuch's demise but I am unsure how exactly. Or perhaps the Emperor got wind of the rumoured plot involving Po Cheng. I don't know. It all happened very quickly. The Emperor does not know his own mind, every wind blows him this way and that." She bowed her head. "Po Cheng was executed this morning. I cannot say I will miss him but I did not wish him such an end. My husband is devastated, believing that Po Cheng was executed in his stead."

"I am sorry we have brought such great trouble." Wen put his hand over his heart. "It was not intended."

"It was not your doing, Wen. I have always known that First Minister Jia and the eunuch were at the heart of all that is wrong with the Court and that eventually they would tire of sharing influence over the Emperor. In any case, Emperor Duzong has more important crises on his hands. News has reached us that the besieged city of Xiangyang has fallen to the Mongols. Soon, it is feared they will begin to move on the capital itself."

"Then perhaps it is a blessing that you and Yang Su are being sent into exile at this time."

"Yes, it is true. We will travel deep into the south to escape the barbarians, perhaps to join your old master. I hope to have time at last to perfect my hand at calligraphy and painting during our time in exile. And you, Wen, what will you and Ming do now? Will you come back to the south with us?"

"I cannot speak for Ming, but I have not yet decided. I know I will not wait here for the Mongols to descend on me. The world, as we know it, is disappearing. The Son of Heaven has failed to protect his people." Wen paused. "Perhaps I will head West, return to the peaks, and wander like a monk of ancient times. Through my art, I have tried to learn how to 'enter the mountains', but to truly enter them, one cannot bring anything along, nothing at all, not even a self. I have more cutting and polishing to do."

Lady Yang nodded. "And you, Ming?" She smiled at him sadly.

Ming took a gold coin from his pocket and turned it shimmering before their eyes. On one side, a dragon; on the other, the face of a lady.

"Ah," Wen shook his head. "I always wondered if you would one day head back to find that tomb with its gold and jade. What would you do with all that wealth, Ming? You would either become dissolute in trying to spend it, or wasted and disturbed in protecting it. Either way, sadly, it would be your ruin."

"No, you misunderstand, my good friend. I have no desire to return to that place. I return for something else. The girl from my town who rescued us from the tomb – not for one moment has she been absent from my mind."

"So, those times you studied my paintings late at night when you thought I slept – were you not searching for the way back to the tomb?"

A look of shock and amazement crossed Ming's face. "You knew?"

"Of course."

"I did not realize…. My deepest apologies, but it was my only means to remember the way back to my town, to where my honourable parents are buried. The tomb was an important marker along the trail, yes, but not my final destination. I will return to Jinhan and find the girl."

Li Wen bowed. "My turn for apologies, dear Ming. I have truly misjudged your purity of heart. Your steadfast loyalty helped me through many a difficult situation and I am sure I will miss it sorely in the future. Parting from you will not be easy. May you reach the home of your ancestors with ease, and I wish you luck in finding the girl in Jinhan."

A silence descended upon them, deepened by the sound of a breeze in the leaves of a gingko tree on the edge of the courtyard, the melancholy call of a bird in the distance.

"And my paintings?" Addressing Lady Yang, Wen held his fingers around his tea cup and stared down into its dark mirror. "Are they destroyed?"

"No. The gods have seen fit to save them. The paintings have been placed in the Emperor's Inner Storage. No one but His Excellency may see them but they are safe. The Son of Heaven was unsure about the arguments put forward by the eunuch that your paintings bore messages of dissent and treason. However, the Emperor was swayed by the eunuch's suggestion, supported by First Minister Jia, that you be killed so that no other sovereign anywhere could have such magnificent paintings in his possession. In the end, the Emperor also feared it would be tempting fate to destroy paintings that were offered as a long-life gift. Remember, the Emperor's greatest obsession, his overweening interest, is his pursuit of immortality." She smiled sadly with her eyes. "Your paintings, Wen, are the very spirit of China. One cannot destroy mountains and rivers. They alone are immortal."

They paused and finished their tea. With a deep heartfelt sigh, Lady Yang said: "I must return now to my husband. There is much to do to prepare for our journey."

Wen and Ming accompanied Lady Yang to the gate where her servant waited. At the gate, Wen bowed. "For the rest of my days, I will never forget the magnificent generosity offered to a poor painter and his peasant friend. Give our greetings, our farewell and much thanks to Yang Su."

Not wanting to prolong the leave-taking, Lady Yang said her final goodbyes. "Farewell, my friends. I hope we will meet again someday." With that, she made her way through the gate to her waiting chair and porters.

Late in the night, Wen rose from sleep, lifted his pack and headed into the meditation hall, finding his way by a brushstroke of moonlight across the floor. Taking a sheet of paper from his pack, he knelt and smoothed it out where the light could illuminate it. Gazing at the sheet, he let the glowing potency of its emptiness enter him.

He drew a medium-sized brush from his pack and held it before his eyes. It was a fine brush, with bristles soft to the touch, its shape simple and smooth, its waist narrow, its black-wood handle shining with reflected moonlight.

Placing the brush on the floor, the tip resting on a small porcelain plate, he lifted his turtle shell, added water from a small pitcher and began grinding a shimmering pool of ink. The ink glowed silver-black in the moonlight and he noticed its distinctive scent emanating from the shell cupped in his palm. He stared at it. *Like blood. Black, luxurious blood.*

The brush felt natural in his hand. He was nearly intoxicated with the smell of the ink as it drew his hand down, the brush penetrating the viscous liquid, which soaked into the lush hairs.

He extended his arm, held the brush horizontally toward the heavens, and bowed; bending his elbow, he touched the brush tip to the tip of his tongue, marking the tongue with a black sigil of ink. The taste was distinctive, earthy.

Raising the brush in the air, Wen brought it straight down forcefully toward the page, stopping as it just touched the paper, the ink pooling into a small liquid dot.

He could feel the landscape of China, mountains and rivers without end, flowing from heaven, through the brush and onto the page.

The dawn awoke with the sounding of the temple gong. Ming had planned to leave early, to begin the long journey back to his home village.

Making his way into the empty meditation hall, Ming spotted the painting on the floor. At the bottom of the painting, he noticed a willow tree. *What was it Wen told me about willow trees? A symbol of...* His breath caught as he remembered.

Running, Ming crossed the courtyard and swung open the gate. The morning was cool and damp with dew, and the leaves of the nearby forest were speckled with birdsong and sunlight.

He hurried to the base of the mountain trail that curled high above the monastery. Gazing up, he could barely discern Wen, already walking the mountain path, his pack bristling with paintbrushes. He was too distant for Ming to give chase or even cry out. Ming watched him rise steadily along the trail. Eventually Wen was so distant, he hardly appeared to be moving at all.

∽

An unsigned note on the curator's desk – *We finally have space for Li Wen's landscapes. I will come by to get the paintings this afternoon.*

The curator of Chinese art considers Li Wen's paintings one last time, gazing at the four seasons as if they are one work, remembering how completely he had disappeared in those mountains. He is saddened by the thought that Li Wen's paintings will fade, as all things fade. *Only mountains last, the mountains and the rivers that course through them. And when Li Wen's paintings are displayed in the museum they will fade even faster. People will come to admire his art and, in their admiration, ultimately destroy it.*

Those who love it will love it to death.

After a few moments, the curator notices something curious about the painting of autumn. From his desk drawer, he retrieves his jeweller's loupes.

He knows Li Wen was hardly more than a tiny cursive brush-stroke of ink in the towering landscape, no larger than a grain of black rice, but now he can't find him.

The curator inspects the other paintings as well. The artist is nowhere to be found. Li Wen has vanished.

Acknowledgements

Deepest thanks for invaluable editorial advice to: Tom Henighan, Nicola Vulpe, Bud and Ann Frutkin (my brother and sister-in-law), and especially Faith Seltzer, my lovely wife and dear accomplice. Thanks also to my persevering and dogged agent, Carolyn Swayze; and perceptive editor for the press, Andrew Steinmetz.

Thanks is due also to the Royal Ontario Museum, for the depth and delights of its Chinese collection, and for granting me access to the stacks of the ROM's H. H. Mu Far Eastern Library; and to my long-time friend, Murray Wilson, for many delightful and engaging discussions on Chinese language and characters, calligraphy and art. Thanks also to Paul Sharp for assistance concerning Chinese characters.

Numerous books and web sites were consulted in the research for this novel. A few of the most important were: *Poetry and Painting in Song China: The Subtle Art of Dissent* (Alfreda Murck), the source of many of the details concerning scholarly dissent in Song paintings (and thanks to *anonymous* for bringing this book to my attention); *The Arts of China* (Michael Sullivan); *New Discoveries in China* (Danielle and Vadime Ellesseeff); *Three Thousand Years of Chinese Painting* (numerous contributors); *The Dynasties of China* (Bamber Gascoigne); *How to Read Chinese Paintings* (Maxwell K. Hearn), a gift from the above-mentioned Murray Wilson; *The Collected Poems of Li He* (and dozens of other collections and anthologies of Chinese poetry); *Science and Civilization in China* (Joseph Needham); *Brilliant Strokes* (Ka Bo Tsang); *The Age of Confucian Rule: The Song Transformation of China* (Dieter Kuhn); *Treasures of the Chinese Scholar* (Fang Jing Pei); *The Eastern Gate* (Janet Gaylord Moore);

Along the Riverbank (Maxwell K. Hearn / Wen C. Fong); *Masterpieces of Chinese Art* (Rhonda and Jeffrey Cooper); *Chinese Calligraphy* (Chen Tingyou); *The Art of East Asia* (Konemann), *Record of the Listener* (Hong Mai), the *Inner Chapters* of Chuang Tsu, the *Tao Te Ching* of Lao Tsu, and many others.

The text for the wall poster in the city of Jinhan, concerning human sacrifice, comes from *The Enlightened Judgments of Ch'ing-ming Chin* (McKnight and Liu).

Most essential and helpful was Jacques Gernet's *Daily Life in China on the Eve of the Mongol Invasion (1250-1276)*, which provided innumerable details about the city of Linan. It was in this volume that I discovered the existence of eating houses in the Southern Song capital that were known to serve human flesh.

ESPLANADE
Books
THE FICTION SERIES AT VÉHICULE PRESS

[Andrew Steinmetz, editor]

A House by the Sea : A novel by Sikeena Karmali

A Short Journey by Car : Stories by Liam Durcan

Seventeen Tomatoes : Tales from Kashmir : Stories by Jaspreet Singh

Garbage Head : A novel by Christopher Willard

The Rent Collector : A novel by B. Glen Rotchin

Dead Man's Float : A novel by Nicholas Maes

Optique : Stories by Clayton Bailey

Out of Cleveland : Stories by Lolette Kuby

Pardon Our Monsters : Stories by Andrew Hood

Chef : A novel by Jaspreet Singh

Orfeo : A novel by Hans-Jürgen Greif
[Translated by Fred A. Reed]

Anna's Shadow : A novel by David Manicom

Sundre : A novel by Christopher Willard

Animals : A novel by Don LePan

Writing Personals : A novel by Lolette Kuby

Niko : A novel by Dimitri Nasrallah

Stopping for Strangers : Stories by Daniel Griffin

The Love Monster : A novel by Missy Marston

A Message for the Emperor : A novel by Mark Frutkin

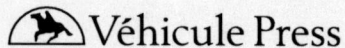